Saving Grace

PRISCILLA CUMMINGS

DUTTON CHILDREN'S BOOKS

NEW YORK

j
cun

C H

Library of Congress Cataloging-in-Publication Data
Cummings, Priscilla, date.
Saving Grace / Priscilla Cummings.
p. cm.
Summary: When Grace's family is evicted from their Washington, D.C.,
apartment just before Christmas 1932, and she and her younger brothers
are sent to a mission, Grace wonders what will become of her sick older brother,
her pregnant mother, and her out-of-work father.
ISBN 0-525-47123-5
[1. Family life—Washington (D.C.)—Fiction. 2. Depressions—1929—Fiction.
3. Washington (D.C.)—Fiction.] I. Title.
PZ7.C9149 Sav 2003   [Fic]—dc21   2002031539

Published in the United States by Dutton Children's Books,
a division of Penguin Young Readers Group
345 Hudson Street, New York, New York 10014
www.penguinputnam.com

Designed by Gloria Cheng
Printed in USA
First Edition
1 3 5 7 9 10 8 6 4 2

With love,
to the memory of my mother-in-law,
Mary Prudence Louise Shannon Frece
(1908–1995)

And also,
with affection and gratitude,
to Betty Dell Stone Stults

Acknowledgments

For sharing their poignant memories of the Great Depression, I have many people to thank, but especially Richard and Minette McCullough. For their insights into the deaf world, I am grateful to Donna Salamoff, Lisa Agogliati, Sarah Segal, and Alicia Balzar, all of whom I met through the Deaf Access Program at BAPA's (Bethesda Academy of Performing Arts) Imagination Stage. Stanley C. Baker, superintendent/principal of the Maryland School for the Deaf, was helpful as well. My thanks to Elsie Wood, historian for the Central Union Mission of Washington, D.C., and to staff members at the Martin Luther King Jr. Library in Washington, D.C., as well as the Nimitz Library of the U.S. Naval Academy in Annapolis, Maryland (my hometown), where I spent an entire summer reading through the microfilm of 1932 newspapers. Finally, I thank my children, William and Hannah, and my husband, John W. Frece, who is always supportive and whose grandmother and mother prompted this story.

Sow a thought and you reap a deed.

Sow a deed and you reap a habit.

Sow a habit and you reap a character.

Sow a character and you reap a destiny.

—Sign posted on the dining-room wall of a camp for needy children
run by the Central Union Mission of Washington, D.C.,
during the Great Depression, 1930s

CONTENTS

SAVING GRACE

A Knock at the Door

When the carved wooden clock that was Grandma Rosa's in Germany "cuckooed" five times in the predawn darkness, Grace knew it was time to get up. Instead, she snuggled deeper into the cushions of the living-room couch and pulled two gray woolen blankets up over her chin. Even with her coat and all her clothes on, Grace felt the bite of cold winter air. She looked forward to getting her hands around a good hot cup of coffee.

A warm drink with a wisp of steam in her face . . . It was not the only thing on Grace's mind as she shifted her foot to avoid the sharp spring that protruded from the back of the couch. Every morning when she awoke, eleven-year-old Grace pressed her lips together and wondered: Would this be the day?

Recently, there had been signs. Down in the dusty furnace room, where she sat cross-legged on the hard stone floor with three other children from the apartment building, Grace had watched the Ouija board mysteriously predict that she would have a new life. And in church last Sunday the Reverend Saunders had raised his fist—*and* his voice—and warned that a thunderous day of reckoning was coming. Despite the apprehension this aroused in others, Grace was positive that a day of reckoning would reward a poor, suffering family like hers. At the very least, she figured, a day of reckoning would come with a warm meal in the heated parish hall.

But as she listened on that dark December morning in 1932, there was not the tiniest ripple of thunder. Only the muted rattle of a milk truck down the avenue outside. And then the sound of Grace's mother in the kitchen, striking a match to start a fire in the gas stove. Grace wondered why she hadn't heard the floor creak when Mama tiptoed through the living room and hoped it didn't mean that her mother had spent the night sitting at the kitchen table, waiting for Papa again.

In the small, one-bedroom apartment where Grace and her family had lived crowded together for the past year, a tiny sliver of winter moonlight filtered through a cracked window facing the alley, and Grace could make out the bulky form of her older brother, Pete, who lay curled up on a tattered feather mattress, on the floor. Pete murmured something in his sleep and, as Grace watched him roll over, hugging a single quilt tightly around his shoulders, an unsettled feeling slowly pulled at her inside.

What else about today had she forgotten? It was Saturday— no school, she remembered with a slight but tentative smile. They were out for the holidays. So, after the chores were done this morning, she could play with Mary Orlinsky. Couldn't she?

Maybe. Mary was three years older, and sometimes she didn't let Grace play. "I hear your mother calling you," she'd singsong to Grace when she and Hallie, who was older, too, wanted to smoke cigarettes with the boys down by the garbage cans. But Mary had a clothesline jump rope, and often there was need for an extra hand:

Ice-cream soda,
Delaware punch,
Tell me the name of your honey bunch. . . .

Pete coughed once, and Grace's smile faded as she remembered that he had asked for her help. "It's a *secret mission*," he had warned with uplifted eyebrows and a sparkle in his deep brown eyes. But Grace knew where he was taking her, and a familiar knot began to form in her stomach.

Suddenly, a soft pool of light from a kerosene lamp spilled into the living room, where Grace and all the children slept. Mama in her nightgown, a shawl around her shoulders, had come quietly to the doorway and made a wide, dark silhouette. "Grace, Pete—it's time to get up," she said in a hushed voice so as not to wake the two younger boys sleeping foot to foot on a cot behind Pete. "Come on. You know Mr. O'Hare doesn't wait around all morning."

Pete moaned, and Grace rubbed the sleep from her eyes.

"Move along, the both of you. Pull on your shoes and grab the buckets at the front door," their mother urged. "I'll have some coffee and grilled bread by the time you're done."

Reluctantly, Grace pushed herself up. Pete slowly stretched an arm over his head but then began to cough again so hard he had to roll back over on his side until his lungs had cleared.

The noise caused four-year-old Owen to stir and yank a shared comforter from his little brother, Iggy.

Mama fixed the cover on the two boys, then knelt over Pete with the lantern. Long, wavy chestnut hair spilled over her shoulders. "That cough sounds awful," she said, placing her hand on his back. "When I get the kettle going this morning, I want you to sit in the steam for a while."

"I'm all right, Ma," Pete protested. He took a deep breath and let it out slowly. "See? It's just a cold."

But Mama bit her lip uncertainly.

"Come on, Gracie, let's go," Pete said, standing up and shivering as he tucked in his shirt beneath his jacket.

Mama stood with him. Pete was only thirteen, but already he was an inch taller than his mother.

"I'm sorry to send you out so early," Mama said. "We've got to have the water, though. I expect Mrs. Hewitt's son has already dropped off her wash downstairs. Saturday is always a big one for her."

Grace pushed her blankets to one side and slid off the couch onto the cold wood floor, where she had left her boots and the two pieces of cardboard cut from the Post Toasties box. She felt the cardboard to see if it had dried overnight, but it was still damp. Disappointed, Grace stuffed the pieces back into the toes of the small black leather boots, where they covered the growing holes in the soles. The cardboard was bumpy; Grace hated the feel of it. But it was better than nothing—and definitely better than wet woolen stockings.

When she finished lacing up her boots, she felt with her hand under the couch to be sure that her treasure box was still there, well hidden from the sticky, prying fingers of Iggy and Owen. It was just an old cigar box, covered with a piece of red velvet left over from a winter cape Aunt Emma had made for herself. But the box was special to Grace. Inside were all the precious things she owned, as well as the list. No one else knew about the list—except, of course, Pete.

"Bundle up, it's cold out there," Mama warned, holding the light over Pete's shoulder as he lifted a scarf from the peg inside the front door and stepped into his boots.

Grace knelt to tie the laces on Pete's boots. She did this for him every day because he only had the one good arm.

"Cold out *there*? It's cold in here!" Pete's teeth chattered as he wrapped the scarf around his neck and waited for Grace to finish.

"I know. It'll warm up, though—as soon as I get the big wash kettle going in the kitchen," Mama reassured him.

After pulling a wool hat over long tangles of thick brown hair, Grace fished in her pockets for the two mismatched mittens that kept her hands warm.

With one finger, Mama tucked several loose strands of hair beneath the edge of Grace's hat. "I heard yesterday we might see some snow today."

Grace's face lit up. "Really?! Enough to go sliding?"

"Maybe." Mama shrugged, but there was a rare and welcome glimmer in her eye because they shared a special passion for snow. One of Grace's earliest memories was of kneeling with her mother on the parlor sofa, back in the old house, and pushing aside the lace curtains to watch the white flakes falling.

"Can we go to the Capitol and coast down the big hill?"

"Oh, my, Grace. That's quite a hike from here, now that we've moved."

"It ain't that far!" Grace exclaimed.

Mama winced at the bad grammar and shushed Grace with a finger to her lips. "It *isn't* that far," she corrected, whispering so as not to wake the boys.

"*Please,* Mama," Grace begged. "It *isn't* that far. Can't we go?"

"Well, maybe Pete can take you." Mama patted her enormous belly to remind Grace of the baby. "It wouldn't be the best thing for me just now."

"Pa coming?" Pete asked. "He going to help us haul water?"

Mama's face clouded. She gathered her shawl close around her shoulders. "No, Pete. He didn't get much sleep last night."

At least he was home, Grace thought. Sometimes he didn't come back until the morning, and it worried Mama sick. He would tell them he found work unloading freight all night in the train yards, then lay out a couple dollars beside a bag of doughnuts on the table. But Grace and Pete knew that's not where he went because they had followed him once.

"Those buckets are heavy," Pete complained.

"Shhhhhh," Mama warned again. "You'll wake Iggy and Owen."

"We'll have to make ten trips if it's just the two of us," he told her.

"There was a meeting last night," Mama tried to explain. "Some of the men are talking about another hunger march. Up in Montgomery County this time. The meeting was important, and it ran late. Your father needs to sleep."

Pete forgot about the heavy buckets. "If there's another hunger march, *I'm* going this time," he insisted.

"Oh no, you're not," Mama disagreed. "The Montgomery police have some horrible new thing called tear gas."

"Can that kill you?" Grace asked.

Mama shook her head. "No, but it hurts your eyes. Real bad."

"I don't understand," Pete cut in, whispering harshly. "Papa said he and the others had a right to protest. That it was free speech."

"The police are afraid things will get out of hand," Mama said.

"Out of hand?" Pete got puffed up with anger quick, like Papa. "If Franklin Roosevelt was in the White House, this wouldn't happen, would it?"

Mama remained calm. "God knows we all want things to change, Pete. But Mr. Roosevelt won't be the president until the inauguration—in March."

Pete's mouth became a tight line. "Hoover's not doing a thing for us! Not a thing!"

"Come *on*, Pete," Grace urged, shoving a bucket at her brother. "We need to get going."

Reluctantly, Pete took the bucket and slapped the wool cap on his head. Mama followed them out the door and stood holding the lantern over the banister so they could see to get started down two dark flights of stairs.

As they passed by closed doors in the narrow hallways, Grace could hear the sounds of other families waking up: their yawning, sleepy voices; a baby crying; pots banging—and from one lucky unit, the crackle and smell of bacon frying. At the bottom of the steps, they saw a basket of laundry.

"Is that for Ma?" Pete asked.

Grace nodded and wrinkled her nose because it appeared to be linens and towels. Towels soaked up so much water, they took a long time to dry.

A door opened ahead of them, and Mr. Ferguson limped into the hallway with his own two pails. He set them in his son's wagon and nodded "good morning." Pete gave Grace his bucket so he could help the older man lower the wagon down the front stairs to the sidewalk.

As she walked behind them, Grace thought about how much Mr. Ferguson had changed in the year they had known him. When her family first moved into the apartment building, just after Papa lost his job with the electric company, Mr. Ferguson was the first real friend they had. He used to tease Grace and her mother all the time about their matching brown braids and freckles. "Two bonnie lasses," he called them, even though Mama wasn't Scottish at all. She was German, which made Grace and Pete part German, too, only they had to swear never to tell anyone.

"People don't like Germans because of the Great War," Mama once explained. "Some Americans won't even call sauerkraut by its rightful name because it's German. They call it *liberty cabbage*."

Grace didn't think Mr. Ferguson would ever hold it against Mama that she was German. He and Papa, who came from Scotland, too, used to play their fiddles together. People gathered in the street to stomp their feet and clap their hands whenever they played. Someday Papa was going to teach Grace how to play the fiddle, too. He had promised he would. Someday. It's just that there hadn't been much music lately. Leastways, not since Mr. Ferguson lost his job, too. No one had to tell her; Grace knew that fetching water this way was embarrassing for him. As it was for everyone unable to pay their bills on time.

Most of the tenants had been without water and electricity for more than a week. It was a wonder, they all said, that the gas for their stoves hadn't been shut off. But they were braced for that, too.

Threatening notices had been pushed under their doors weeks ago. Harsh letters in bold black ink that warned if families didn't pay their rent in thirty days, they would be turned out onto the street. Papa balled up the paper and threw it in the trash. "I'd like to see 'em try!" he had railed. But Mama had murmured how now "we'll all live in fear of every knock at the door."

"Come on, Gracie, hurry up!" Pete urged her.

Grace picked up her pace. She could smell the coming snow in the air.

On the street corner a block away, Mr. O'Hare from the fire department had the fire hydrant opened, and people without running water were already filling their buckets for the day. Grace and Pete would have to hurry. It wasn't enough to just fill the two buckets they had. That would be barely enough for coffee and soup and flushing the toilets. They had to get several more bucketfuls so that Mama could do Mrs. Hewitt's wash, too.

The fireman grinned at them from under his enormous handlebar mustache and rubbed his hands together to get them warm. "Mornin' there, Miss Grace. Mornin', Peter," he greeted in his thick Irish brogue.

"Good morning," Grace replied. Her breath made a cloud in the still, frigid air.

She gave Mr. O'Hare her bucket and watched as he filled it halfway with water that gushed from the hydrant. Half a bucket was all she could lift.

Pete touched his cap in greeting and, because of his bad arm, let Mr. O'Hare fill his bucket, too. Pete could carry the water home with his left hand. It was just his right arm that was useless. He was born with it that way, an arm that stopped at elbow length with a deformed hand. Most days he kept it covered, but in the summer, when it was too hot for long sleeves, the alley boys teased. "Gimp!" they called him. Martin Jeeter was the worst. "Are you a secretary? We see you take *shorthand*!"

"Peter." Mr. O'Hare put a hand on Pete's shoulder. "The chief's been gettin' some complaints about opening the hydrant here. We'll be needin' to curtail it."

"When?" Pete asked, concerned. "When will you stop?"

The fireman appeared grim. "We'll try to keep it going a couple more days. For you people here in the apartments. But you've got to understand, son, we're not authorized to be doing this."

"We've *got* to have water!" Pete argued.

Mr. O'Hare nodded in sympathy, but he didn't say anything more.

Afraid of what this meant, Grace watched as Pete dropped his hand against his side and then abruptly turned away from Mr. O'Hare.

"Come on, let's go," he told her. "It'll be all right."

But Grace had caught the look in her brother's eyes.

As she began to lug her bucket back to the apartment, water sloshed over the edge and ran down one stocking into Grace's boot. Suddenly overcome by the load, she set the bucket down to switch hands and didn't notice that the first snowflakes had begun to fall.

SURVIVAL

Y ou dirty bloodsuckers! Outta here!"

Papa's voice was so loud that even outside the apartment building Grace and Pete could hear every word he hollered.

"Clement, *please*! Don't break anything!" Mama shouted.

A loud crash followed. Grace could hear Iggy and Owen start crying. She and Pete set their buckets down and dashed inside the building, where they smelled smoke and saw a frightened woman peering through a crack in a first-floor doorway. Upstairs, someone screamed.

"Pete, wait!" Grace cried, rushing after him. Halfway to the first landing, however, she and Pete were stopped by three big men with tight woolen caps and grim, unshaven faces who tromped heavily down the stairs toward them.

"Back up, Grace." Pete put a protective arm in front of his sister as they pressed themselves against the wall.

After the men brushed past, Grace and Pete raced up the rest of the stairs. An overturned wash kettle sat in the hallway, and Papa's club lay on the doorsill. Papa always kept the club hidden under his bed pillow in case of an intruder, but neither Pete nor Grace had ever seen him use it.

Pete picked up the club; then he and Grace hurried into the kitchen, where Papa was wrapping a towel around the handle of a smoking skillet.

"Calm yourself, Clement, before someone gets hurt," Mama begged, breathless, as she sat and put both hands on her belly. Iggy struggled to climb into her lap while, under the table, Owen sucked his thumb and watched with wide eyes.

"What happened?" Pete asked. "Did you hit someone, Pa?"

"I *should* have!" Papa snapped as he awkwardly settled the hot skillet in an open window. "Those cowards!" He turned, his face red and his eyes flashing angrily. "Threaten me, will they!"

"Clement, *please*," Mama begged, pulling Iggy onto what little lap she had. She turned to Pete and Grace. "No one was hurt. But some men came. They told us to pay the rent by five o'clock or else."

"Or else *what*?" Pete asked.

"They'll throw us out!" Papa erupted again, shaking a fist at the door.

"Clement, the children!" Mama warned.

Papa lowered his hand, but his fist remained clenched.

"Do you think they mean it?" Pete asked.

Their father's anger could not be contained. He pointed an angry finger at Pete. "They'd better not try!"

Pete backed up.

"It's not Pete's fault. Don't yell at *him*!" Mama said firmly, her arms wrapped around Iggy.

The room fell silent except for Iggy's whimpering.

Papa dropped his head. "I'm not yellin' at Pete," he denied in a weak voice.

"Mama, will we pay?" Grace asked.

"We can't," she said quietly. "There's no money. Not a red cent."

"Where will we go, then?" Grace asked anxiously.

"Nowhere!" Papa burst out again, so loudly—and so suddenly this time—that Iggy buried his face in Mama's neck. Owen scooted farther beneath the table. "I told them bloody buggers if they set a foot in this apartment, I'd do sorry business with them!"

"Clement, *please*," Mama pleaded again. "You're *scaring* the children!"

But Papa's anger continued to boil now. He didn't used to be this way, but now Grace worried every time he got really upset that he'd lash out at someone, or punch another hole in the plaster wall. She knew he didn't mean to hurt anyone or cause any damage, but sometimes he got so angry he couldn't help himself. The last time he hit the wall with his fist so hard he scraped the skin off his knuckles and broke a finger. Mama and Grace taped up the hand with strips torn from a pillowcase, but the finger never did mend right.

Papa threw down the towel in his hands, grabbed his coat, and stomped out, his footsteps echoing as he went down the stairs.

Mama sighed, as she always did when he left, because it was at once a relief *and* a worry because no one ever knew when Papa would be back. Every day he went out looking for work, sometimes returning with only a couple nickels for bread and oatmeal, a few potatoes maybe. Every once in a while he'd be gone all night—unloading freight, so he said—and the pay was better. But more often he came back hollow-eyed and empty-handed, and everyone went to bed hungry.

Iggy stopped crying and, in the quiet that followed Papa's departure, Pete told his mother about the water. "Mr. O'Hare said he'd try to keep the hydrant open another couple of days."

Mama's tired eyes stared at a far corner of the room. "What next?" she mumbled.

Grace and Pete looked at each other, then at the table, where Mama had set out for each of them a solitary piece of bread grilled in lard and salt and a cup of black coffee.

Pete swallowed. "It's not my turn to eat today," he reminded her.

"Go ahead," Mama told him.

Pete didn't argue. Eagerly, he reached over to scoop up the bread. "Maybe Aunt Em and Uncle Stewart could give us water." He ate hungrily.

Grace took the bread from her plate, too. It tasted good even if it was so stale it was hard to chew.

Mama didn't respond, so Grace and Pete, still eating, left to retrieve their water buckets from in front of the apartments.

Outside, Grace stared up the sidewalk into the hazy gray light of early morning, hoping to spot her father. She saw him crossing the street a block away and couldn't help but remember the night last spring when she and Pete had followed him. All they wanted were some of the doughnuts Papa brought home from the train yard. But the train yard was not where

Papa went. Instead, Grace and Pete followed him back to their old neighborhood nearly three miles away, where he disappeared into a neighbor's house.

"Shhhh. Be quiet," Pete had warned, taking Grace's hand as they crept, picking their way beneath the branches of a fragrant lilac bush. Flat on the ground they lay, spying through the little basement window beside the coal chute. They could only catch glimpses of what was going on. A big pot. Glass bottles lined up. Corn. "Holy crow!" Pete had whispered urgently. "They're making liquor, Grace. Bootleg!"

"What's wrong with that?"

"It's against the law," Pete had told her. "If the cops find out, they'll arrest everybody. They'll throw Papa in jail!"

"Why's he doin' it, then?"

"What do you think? To make money. *Survival*," he'd said.

Grace would never forget how scared she was, hiding in the dark by the coal chute. But what happened later, when they got caught, was far worse; she couldn't bear to think back on it, not even in the safety of her own mind.

"Grace, you're daydreaming!" Pete accused, turning around to wait for her to catch up with her bucket. "Come *on*! We got work to do."

With others from the building they retraced their steps several times, trudging silently back and forth to the hydrant for buckets of water that they dumped into Mama's wash kettle. Grace kept switching hands, but the metal buckets were heavy. They pulled on her shoulders and banged into her shins. Water kept spilling over the edge, down her stockings;

and her hands hurt, too, as the cold, wet mittens began to freeze against her skin.

"Here, here, that'll do," Mama finally said.

Grace winced as she peeled the stiff, wet wool from her pink fingers. Shakily, she held her hands up in front of the stove.

"When you're done, come help me sort," Mama said, eager to get the wash started.

Grace opened and closed her hands several times and left the stove to kneel on the floor by the laundry. Sorting was a job she did with some fervor because once, while checking the pockets of Mr. Hewitt's pants, she had found a gold pocket watch. There was barely a moment of indecision before Grace slid the timepiece into her boot. Later she and Pete pawned the watch for five dollars. They used the money for emergencies, such as nights Papa didn't come home and they needed food—even if it was just a loaf of bread and a tin of condensed milk.

The pocket watch is what got them started. Pete never let Grace call it stealing. "A loan. It's a *loan*," Pete had insisted, fixing his eyes on hers. "Write it down on this piece of paper and keep it in that box of yours," he said. "Someday we'll pay everyone back."

Mama stood with her arm stretched out. "Grace," she said impatiently. "That tablecloth—would you hand it up to me?"

Grace handed her the cloth, and Mama dropped it into the big wash kettle on the stove, where she scrubbed the linens on a washboard. Afterward, Grace rinsed everything in a second kettle, then wrung out the linens over the sink and hung them with wooden clothespins on the line that ran from the fire escape landing to the building across the alleyway. Sometimes things froze on the line or got to smelling bad from all the garbage cans and smoke from fires that derelicts lit in the alley down below. Frozen clothes and towels could be whacked and pulled in, but God forbid they got smelly, because then Grace and Mama would have to start all over again.

Once the laundry was dry, Mama would press everything on the kitchen table with flat irons she heated on the gas stove. All of which was a lot of work for her and Grace. But Mrs. Hewitt paid seventy-five cents for every basket of wash. And seventy-five cents bought a lot of groceries at the Piggly Wiggly: a dozen eggs, a loaf of bread, two pounds of lard, and a bag of flour. Maybe even a few horehound drops for the kids.

Mama stood with her sleeves rolled up and her hands on her hips, surveying what was left of the laundry. She had braided her hair and pulled it back into a rounded bun at the nape of her neck, but long, curly tendrils had broken loose and clung to the edges of her damp, round face. "We'll do the rest later," she said, pushing the hair away from her eyes. "I need to wash some of Iggy's diapers."

Grace watched with a dip in her heart as Mama sucked in her breath and stretched tall with her hands against her back. Grace knew it was a sin to think this, but sometimes she wished there was not a new baby coming. She dearly wanted a baby sister. With three brothers already, she *needed* a sister. A cute little girl with brown ringlets named Lillian or Lucille, because then they could call her Lily or Lucy. She would be a live doll baby to push around in Iggy's battered pram. A little friend Grace could cut out paper dolls for and play jacks with on the warm summer sidewalks at dusk.

But Grace knew it was not a good time for another baby. Not even a sweet little girl they called Lily or Lucy. She lowered her eyes and piled the unwashed towels back into the basket.

While she and Mama worked, Iggy and Owen rolled a metal car around the cold, bare wooden floor of the kitchen. "Careful!" Mama warned them over and over when they got too close to the stove.

"Iggy's got a stinkie," Grace said, wrinkling her nose when she got a whiff of the little boy's diaper.

Pete, meanwhile, cleaned the kerosene lanterns, trimmed the wicks, then left to see if Mr. Tom at the corner newsstand needed help hawking newspapers.

"I wish *I* could go," Grace said enviously as she watched the door close behind him. She never forgot how last May Pete made fifteen cents selling "Extra" newspapers when Amelia Earhart flew alone in an airplane across the Atlantic Ocean— the first woman to do it.

"I need you here, darlin'," Mama said sweetly. "Help me empty this kettle, would you? Then you can change Iggy for me and we'll do something with that hair."

Grace grabbed a handful of the thick brown hair that fell to her waist, twisted it, and tossed it back over her shoulder before helping Mama hoist the wash kettle. When they were done, she changed Iggy and, holding her nose, quickly dropped the messy cloth diaper into a tin pail on the fire escape.

"Nothing exciting," Pete complained when he returned a few minutes later, hanging up his hat on a peg in the kitchen. "An automobile accident in Silver Spring. A murder at the racetrack up in Laurel."

Grace moved her hands around in the kettle's warm rinse water.

"Plus a guy stuck his head in a gas oven and committed suicide on account of he lost his job and couldn't support his wife—"

"Enough, Pete!" Mama cut him off. She eyed him sternly. "Watch the boys while I do Grace's hair."

Grace wondered how sticking your head in a gas oven could kill you but knew this wasn't the time to ask. Drying her hands on her dress, Grace went to sit on her mother's bed. When Mama came in, Grace handed the brush backward over her shoulder, bracing herself for a vigorous brushing. Mama was surprisingly gentle, however; silent, too, as she braided Grace's hair.

Grace loved the feel of her mother's hands as they rhythmically separated thick, silky ropes of hair and wound them together into one long plait that hung down Grace's back. Sometimes her mother sang as she did this. "Beautiful Dreamer" or, Grace's favorite since she was a baby, "Tell Me Why." But there was no singing, no humming this morning.

"Are you worried?" Grace asked.

"About what?"

"Those mean men," Grace said. "The ones who came this morning."

Mama didn't answer right away. While she waited, Grace traced with her index finger the pretty cotton swirls in her mother's chenille bedspread. The bed it covered was special because it once belonged to Grandma Rosa in Germany.

Mama's busy hands brushed the small of Grace's back as they neared the end of the braid. When she finished, she would lean forward to kiss Grace on the neck, and Grace would giggle and scrunch up her shoulders as she always did because she was very ticklish there, behind her ear.

Grace began to smile in anticipation. But there was no kiss this time, just an odd shaking of the bed. When Grace turned around, she saw Mama crying. Fat tears ran down her face, disappearing under the hand she held over her mouth.

Wharton's wrong, Mama?"

Mama pulled Grace close and wrapped her arms around her. "I *am* worried," she confessed. "And I don't know if I can bear up much longer."

Grace hugged her mother back tight, pressing her face into Mama's damp sweaty blouse.

Mama's large body shuddered with her sobs. "Four pieces of bread left . . . nothing for supper."

"Don't worry. *Please*, Mama," Grace pleaded. "I got some money."

Mama stopped crying. "What do you mean?" she asked, slowly releasing Grace.

"I got some money hid," Grace explained. "Pete and me do. It's in my sock, in the cigar box. For emergency!"

Disbelieving, Mama stretched her eyes. "How much have you got, Grace?"

"Twenty cents."

"Twenty cents? You're sure?"

Grace nodded excitedly.

"That's enough for some bread and eggs at the alley store."
With one hand Mama wiped the tears off her cheeks. "And a
bone at the butcher's, too." Her face brightened a little. "I can
make soup. Oh, my, Grace. You *are* my saving grace; you know
that, don't you?"

They hugged each other again. But the moment of peace
was short-lived because Papa was back, slamming the front
door shut. "Ruth!" he called.

"Yes," she replied. "In here!"

"The others say ignore it," Papa told her when they met in
the kitchen. He stomped snow from his shoes. "We've been
threatened before. Those that can will pay. Then they'll leave
us alone."

"You're not worried, then?" Mama asked.

He shook his head no. But Mama did not seem convinced.

Grace hoped they wouldn't argue. "I'm giving Mama twenty
cents," she said quickly.

Papa looked at her. "Twenty cents? Where'd you get twenty
cents?"

"Saved it up!" Grace grinned. It was true, she told herself.
She *had* saved the money—even if it did come from filching
things.

"Well, we're obliged then, Grace."

When Papa sat down to undo his boots, Grace glanced at
Pete, who half smiled at her.

"Some of the men, they're choppin' wood up on Georgia
Avenue this afternoon," Papa said. "Might be able to get a dollar for it."

The likelihood of a dollar, on top of Grace's twenty cents,

was reassuring news indeed. No one would have to go without eating today. Mama turned her attention to lunch and began grilling the rest of the bread.

"Are there any more chores for Pete?" she asked Papa as they pulled in their chairs at the table. "He's cleaned the lanterns for me. He says he and Grace have some plans."

Pete winked at her, but Grace looked away and bit her lower lip. She had hoped he'd forgotten his secret mission.

"I'd like to go right after lunch," Pete said, using a crust from his bread to get the last bit of grease from his plate. "Unless you need me, Pa." More than life itself, Pete hated to do anything that prompted Papa's disapproval.

Papa resumed eating, but Grace knew what he was thinking: that Pete with his one arm wouldn't be any help chopping wood.

"Go ahead," Papa mumbled.

Grace swallowed the last bite and wiped her mouth on her sleeve.

"Your manners, Grace," Mama scolded.

"Sorry," Grace apologized, "but we don't *have* any napkins." She scraped back her chair.

"Where you going now?" Pete asked.

"The lavatory, if you don't mind," Grace told him as she lifted the kerosene lantern near the stove. Mama lit it for her with a match.

In the hallway lavatory, which three families on the second floor shared, Grace closed and latched the door. It always smelled bad in the lavatory, especially now that they couldn't flush very often; and there were no windows, so the tiny room was dark, too. Grace hung the lantern on a hook beside the door, then stepped up on the old Sears Roebuck catalog someone had left on the floor, its pages for use as toilet paper, and stared at her splintered image in the spotted, broken mirror above the sink.

Sometimes Grace felt the way she appeared in this mirror—broken into two different pieces. There was good old Grace, still the biggest part of the mirror: Mama's little helper, big sister to Owen and Iggy, friend to Pete, Papa's "best girl." But there in the other portion of mirror was new Grace. Grace who had to be tough sometimes, if only to fit in with the alley kids. Grace who took things that didn't belong to her.

Grace closed her eyes. Yet another slice of her would have to be labeled Grace the Coward, because more than anything else in the world, more than hunger and being cold and not having a nice dress for school, Grace was afraid of rats. And *that* was the problem, because Pete wanted her to go to the dump and the dump was filled with rats! Sometimes even teeming with rats!

Pete didn't care, though. Rats didn't scare him. "They're just rodents. Big mice," he teased her, running his fingers like tiny mice feet up her arm. All he wanted was to get empty milk bottles to return to the market. Ten bottles earned him a penny. With a dime Pete would buy a hundred marbles, then resell them, five for a penny, to make money for Christmas presents: a cigar for Papa, some ribbon candy for Mama.

But the rats scared Grace. A rat had bitten her once, right through the nail of her big toe, when she was a little girl playing in the woodpile.

And, truth be known, it wasn't just the rats that frightened Grace. There was Martin Jeeter, too. Martin lived near the dump, and he'd threatened that if Pete ever set foot in his neighborhood, he'd bust his jaw.

Of course, nothing ever stopped Pete once he put his mind to it. Grace knew she'd have to go or else Pete would go alone.

Opening her eyes, Grace turned away from her splintered reflection and issued a long sigh.

Outside, the snow had already piled up to an inch, and more was falling. Grace tugged her hat down over her ears and, because her mittens hadn't dried, stuffed her hands in her pockets to keep them warm. Pete walked beside her with his collar turned up against the cold and his hand snug in his pocket, too.

"There's got to be an easier way to make a dime," Grace said, taking a giant step to avoid the sidewalk crack, half covered with snow. She hoped it didn't count as bad luck to step on a crack you couldn't see.

"What are you suggesting, Grace?"

Grace was desperate for an idea. "I don't know," she said. "Couldn't we maybe *take* something instead?"

Pete frowned at her. "*Steal* something, you mean?"

"*Borrow*," Grace retorted. "Borrow and put it on our list."

Pete frowned. "You don't want to actually *become* a thief, do you? A common criminal? Stealing for food, the way we do, it's not the same thing."

Grace's shoulders slumped with disappointment. "Well, it was just a thought," she muttered.

"Yeah, well, you know what Mama says: 'Sow a thought, you reap a deed. Sow a deed, you reap a habit.'"

Grace rolled her eyes. Pete got a little too preachy sometimes. Besides, she never intended to *become* a thief. She knew that she and Pete would pay everybody back someday. Why else would they keep the list? But now she wondered: Did God recognize different rules when it came to stealing?

"Anyway," Pete continued, "I would never buy a Christmas gift with money I got from stealing. It would be on my conscience."

"Hmmpf," Grace grunted. She scuffed through the snow. "Look, I told Mary I'd play later. So I hope we don't have to stay too long in that dump."

"How do I know how long it'll take?" Pete sounded irritated. "Besides, you shouldn't be hanging around with Mary. She's ignorant. She can't speak proper—one reason *you're* using bad grammar—and she's got a dirty mouth besides."

"But she's the only one near my age in the whole building," Grace argued.

Pete scoffed. "If you ask me, *no* friend's better than Mary. Mama says so, too."

Frustrated, Grace kicked a stone when they stopped at the curb to let a car pass.

"By the way," Pete said as they crossed the street, "I know about the Ouija board, Grace. And if Mama knew, she'd have a fit. She thinks that's witchcraft, you know."

"It's just a game!" Grace insisted, although she knew darn well she would stake her life on what the Ouija board said.

"I've seen Mary smoking cigarettes, too," Pete said.

"But they're not real!" Grace exclaimed. "Just scraps of tobacco rolled up in pieces of newspaper!"

Pete stopped to look at her. "How do you know? You tried one?"

"Well, maybe I have and maybe I haven't!" Grace retorted angrily.

"See?" Pete pushed her arm with one finger. "You never would have talked back to me like that before."

Their eyes met, and Grace backed down. She knew Pete was only looking out for her. "Sorry," she mumbled meekly.

"Yeah, well." Pete's voice softened. "Cut it out, will you?"

They walked on.

"Just so you know, though, you're wrong about Mary," Grace ventured. "She's not bad *all* the time, Pete. Sometimes she's nice. *Real* nice. And besides, she tells me stuff."

Pete scowled. "Like *what?*"

"Like *that*," Grace said, stopping Pete and pointing to a sign in a nearby shop window: PALMS READ. "A clairvoyant told Mary what was going to happen in the future. And Mary told me!"

Pete laughed and resumed walking.

"It's not funny, Pete! The clairvoyant's real—her name's Carletta. She read Mary's palm!"

"Hogwash!" Pete snorted.

"It's *not* hogwash!" Grace cried, pulling on Pete's sleeve to slow him down. "Listen to me, Pete! Carletta told Mary that she had a real guardian angel. Not like in the Bible, Pete. But a real one, who might even look like a regular person. Then, when Mary asked about me, Carletta told her *I* had a guardian angel, too."

At that, Pete stopped dead in his tracks and turned to stare at her. "Then where is she? Huh?" He thrust out his hand. "Where is this guardian angel, Grace? And why isn't she down here getting us out of this mess?"

Grace had the answer. "Because she doesn't come until you absolutely need her. *Absolutely!*"

Pete threw back his head. "Geezy, peezy, Grace! What a buncha bunk! Doesn't that just prove how dumb Mary is? I'm sure her mother gave that clairvoyant . . . maybe as much as a *dollar* to read their palms!"

Grace dropped her mouth, stunned to hear that Mary and her mother might have paid so much money.

Pete kept walking. And Grace had to run to catch up with him.

Continuing in silence, they crossed another street, where a skinny stray dog began to follow them. Grace wished she had some soda crackers to give it.

Suddenly, they heard music and stopped. Not far away, a group of carolers sang. *"Deck the halls with boughs of holly! Fa la la la laaaaaa, la la la la."*

Grace had almost forgotten it was nearly Christmas.

"'Tis the season to be jolly. . . ."

Jolly. Grace tried to remember when her family had been jolly. When was the last time they had all laughed together? It sure wasn't last Christmas. Last Christmas there were no gifts—not even a tree, because they were busy packing boxes to move. Christmas Eve they slept on the floor, because all their beds except for Mama's had been sold for grocery money.

Was it the Christmas before then? Grace remembered a turkey for dinner. And Papa holding up the new baby to see the star on top of the tree. Ignatius McFarland, they had named him, but already everyone called him Iggy. Santa Iggy because he had a little Santa Claus hat.

"Are you coming?" Pete called from up ahead.

That Christmas Papa carved a checkerboard from a big piece of wood—and Santa left a metal train under the tree. The boxcars were washed-out Spam cans with bottle-cap wheels and empty thread spools for smokestacks.

They still lived in their house then. The house had a window box full of petunias and a little gate out front that latched. On Sundays, after church, they went fishing down at the Potomac River, near the long bridge to Anacostia. Both Grace and Pete had their own pole. Papa caught a fish once that was so big it filled the entire kitchen sink.

Grace smiled at the memory. Sundays were the best. Sometimes they took the trolley to Griffith Stadium to watch the Washington Senators. It was fun being in the baseball stadium way up high. Once Grace stood up on her seat. "Look," she had told Pete, "you can see the Capitol and all the way down to the Washington Monument!" Disgusted, Pete shook his head. "Yeah, you can see everything but the game," he grumped, because they were stuck behind one of those posts.

If they didn't go fishing or to the game, they might pile into Uncle Stewart's car for a ride. Like out to Bethesda for ice cream. And once to a place called Waverly Beach way out in

Maryland on the Chesapeake Bay. There was a sign posted by the entrance to Waverly Beach: NO NEGROES. NO JEWS.

Silence as they sat in the car. Aunt Emma, who was deaf, had begun to sign frantically. The worry, like all emotions, was exaggerated on her face. Mama signed back and translated for Papa: "Emma says we shouldn't go there if they don't let everyone in." Papa replied, "'Tis true, Emma, but we didn't come all this way for nothin'."

Grace saved a pretty oyster shell from Waverly Beach—NO NEGROES. NO JEWS. She kept the shell in her cigar box. But they never went back.

"Hey! Grace!" Pete called, tearing into the daydream.

Grace blinked and the memories scattered. When had their lives come to this?

"Hurry up!" her brother hollered as he disappeared into the dump.

Grace glanced back over her shoulder to see if the dog was coming, too, but it had put its tail between its legs and was skulking away. She didn't blame it. She'd take off, too, if she could. Even from here Grace could see that, inside the dump, rats were all over the place.

DOWN IN THE DUMPS

Grace froze, planting her two feet close together and curling her cold, bare hands against her chest. A rat was so close, she could see the yellow of its two front teeth. The rats didn't used to be so bold. But now nothing seemed to scare them away. Not hollering, or waving a stick—or throwing an empty can.

Up ahead, Pete waded through a pile of newspapers, kicking aside a rusty bucket and flinging a tattered seat cushion through the air. "Come on, Gracie. The rats won't bite. They're afraid of *you*, remember?"

"Oh, but they're not! Look!" Grace argued, her teeth chattering against the cold as she pointed in front of her.

Pete shook his head, frustrated. "Then don't come next time!"

His tone of voice hurt because Grace loved Pete. She didn't want to let him down. For her help today, Pete was going to give her one of his best shooters—not his blue agate, because Pete would never give away his blue aggie, but one of his clearies, or maybe the yellow cat's-eye she liked.

It wasn't just the marbles, though. Grace didn't want to let Pete down because he was far more to her than just a brother. Sure, he was tough on her sometimes, but he was the most kindhearted person she knew, next to Mama. Not once did Pete ever complain about eating every other day so Grace and the little boys didn't have to go without. He was someone she could talk to. Plus, he looked out for her.

Although he was barely a teenager, Pete was tall for his age. Built hefty—and handsome, too, like Papa, with his dark brown curly hair and piercing brown eyes. And even though he had that bad right arm, he could throw a hard left-handed punch, thanks to lessons from Uncle Stewart, who had once been a professional boxer up in Boston.

Pete was smart, too. Smarter than Papa, Grace suspected, although she would never say that out loud. Papa knew a lot about watts and wires, but he wasn't much with math, or with words. And Pete loved to read.

Last night, when it was too cold to go to sleep, Grace wrapped a blanket around her shoulders and went into the kitchen, where she found Pete with his nose in a book. Teachers were always giving Pete books to read. Pete had a candle lit and used a hammer to hold down the pages.

"What you reading?" Grace had asked.

"A book about Thomas Jefferson. Do you know who he was?"

Grace had scrunched up her nose and guessed. "A president?"

"Third president of the United States, a signer of the Declaration of Independence, *and* an inventor, Grace. That's what I want to be. A famous inventor. Only I want to be rich, too, like John D. Rockefeller. I want to make a million dollars by the time I'm twenty-five years old."

"A million dollars?!" Grace sat down across from him and pulled the blanket snug around her. "What would you do with all that money, Pete?"

"Buy us a house with heat and lights, for one thing," he said.

"Our old house?" Grace asked. She never stopped wishing they would return to the bungalow on Maryland Avenue where she had grown up.

Pete shook his head. "Naw. I'd buy us a big brick house up in Wesley Heights." His eyes widened. "And a brand-new Packard—like the one Uncle Stewart drives for that rich family."

Grace was excited. "With a rumble seat!"

"Shhhhh!" Pete waved his hand at her and lowered his own voice. "When I'm older, when I'm thirty-five, Grace, I'm going to run for president of the United States. Someday, you just wait, I'm going to find a way to make this country a better place—a place where no one who wants to work will ever be without a job."

Pete said it as if it were a fact and Grace was confident it would happen. Someday everyone would know what Grace knew already—that Pete was special. He was going to *be somebody*.

Just thinking about all this gave Grace the resolve to get her frozen feet moving in that cold, stinky dump. She didn't want to be sitting in the White House parlor one day drinking tea while Pete was slapping his knee, laughing, and telling everyone stories about what a scaredy-cat she'd been.

"Hey! Look!" Pete called out, triumphantly holding up a milk bottle.

Startled, Grace slipped backward and squashed a rotten grapefruit that spurted brown juice into the air.

"Good one!" she called back, wincing and hoping none of that stinky juice had gotten on her boots.

Pete was smiling. "Get the bag, Grace!"

While she walked toward Pete, she reached into her coat pocket for the flour sack they used to hold the empty bottles. They placed the bottle inside. From then on Grace stayed close behind her brother as they meandered through canyons of discarded furniture and over hills of garbage, rusted bedsprings, and punctured tires. Even with snow falling, the stench was nauseating. Grace pulled down her sleeve and held one hand over her nose.

"I guess this'll be enough. We need to buy that food and get on home," Pete said, reaching between the rusted frame of a smashed-up bicycle to get one more bottle. It made four altogether. Carrying the flour sack with the bottles clinking, they slowly retraced their slippery steps.

Grace didn't like the alley store. Even though it was warm, the place was dimly lit, musty smelling, and run by people she didn't trust.

"What you kids want?" a stern old man demanded. He picked at his teeth with a jackknife and squinted at them from behind the big cash register.

Bravely, Grace stepped to the counter. "Six slices of bread and four eggs, please."

The man closed his knife. "Yeah? How much money you got?"

Grace hid the coins in her fist. "Ten cents," she lied.

The man raised his eyebrows.

Grace lifted her chin defiantly. If Grace had told him she had fifteen cents, that's what he would charge her. Even though everyone knew you could get a whole loaf of Jumbo Bread for just a nickel at the Piggly Wiggly. But the Piggly Wiggly was a ten-cent streetcar ride away. The alley store was here, in the neighborhood, and it would sell a few slices of bread instead of a loaf, four eggs instead of a dozen. And therein lay the trade-off.

"All right," the man grumbled.

"Four eggs and six slices of bread," Grace repeated, putting two nickels on the counter. When he delivered the items, wrapped in wax paper, Grace carefully set them into the flour sack beside the four empty milk bottles.

"Oh," she said sweetly, feigning surprise. "I didn't realize I had another nickel." Actually, she and Pete had two more nickels, but the other one, for the soup bone, was in Pete's pocket. "I'll take six more slices of bread, please."

The man glowered at her. "Ya little connivers." He pulled out a handful of bread and slapped the slices on the counter. Grace scooped them up and slid her nickel across the counter. When she glanced at Pete, she saw he was watching with a smug expression *and* quietly slipping something into his coat pocket.

As they left the store, Grace glanced longingly at the jaw-breakers and the ropes of black licorice behind glass in a small wooden case. She didn't see Martin Jeeter until she nearly bumped into him.

"It's okay," Pete said when Grace gasped and stepped back. "Just keep walking."

But Martin barred their way. Tall and lanky, with pants too short and coat sleeves that stopped inches above his bony wrists, he stood with his feet a foot apart and crossed his arms. When he smiled, he showed off the hole from his missing front tooth as if he was proud of it.

"How goes it, Mr. Smarty-Pants?" he asked Pete.

Pete touched Grace in the back.

"And what's in the bag?" Martin asked.

"No trouble here!" the man at the cash register warned loudly.

Slowly, Martin stepped aside, just enough so that Pete and Grace could get by. Once outside, they walked fast. All they wanted to do was buy the soup bone and get home. Two blocks away, however, halfway down the alley they cut through, Martin leaned against the side of a building, waiting for them. He wasn't even out of breath. Two other boys stood with him.

"Let's turn around, quick!" Grace said.

"No." Pete stopped her. "We have a right to walk here. I can handle it."

Grace could tell Pete was scared, though. He never held her hand, and now he had it squeezed tightly in his.

"I don't want any trouble, Martin," Pete said.

"I don't want no trouble neither, Gimp. So tell me, what's in the bag?"

"It's none of your business," Pete said firmly.

Martin looked askance at his friends and cocked his head. Instantly, the other two moved into the alley, blocking the way. One of the boys stepped forward and snatched the bag from Grace's hand.

"Give it back, you mealymouthed Okie!" Grace hollered, reaching for her bag.

But the boy swung the bag out of her reach and shoved Grace back.

"Don't you touch her!" Pete snapped, dropping Grace's hand and knocking the boy's arm off his sister with one swift move of his left arm.

"Get him!" Martin ordered.

The boy with the bag dropped it, and Grace heard the bottles break.

"Help! Somebody help!" she hollered as the two boys grabbed Pete and Martin punched him square in the jaw.

Pete wriggled away and lunged at Martin, socking him hard in the stomach. Martin doubled over in pain. But as soon as Pete stepped back, the other two boys jumped him again and threw him to the ground.

Martin straightened up but clutched his stomach. "Stupid Gimp," he said before spitting on Pete. "Roll him!" he ordered.

The boys turned Pete over and checked all of his pockets, taking not only the nickel they found but the pilfered can of sardines from the alley store.

"This'll teach you to be so selfish," Martin said before swinging his foot back and kicking Pete full in the face.

"Stop it!" Grace screamed.

Pete grabbed his nose and moaned.

When Martin lifted his foot to stomp on Pete's bad arm, Grace sprang toward him, hitting him on the chest with both hands. The boys grabbed her, yanking her off, and Martin started to laugh.

Several floors above them, a woman threw open a window. "I'll call the police on you pack of scoundrels!" she yelled down at them.

Martin swung his head around. Someone was entering the alley. "Let's go!" he ordered. The boys released Grace and took off running.

Grace dropped beside Pete, who lay curled up on the frozen ground, still moaning. Dark red blood from his nose made a crimson blossom on the white snow. He struggled to breathe. "My nose, Grace. I think it's broken."

Patting her pockets, Grace searched for something to stem the bleeding but found only her thin handkerchief, which she pressed against Pete's nose.

"Easy," he said.

"Oh, Pete. What are we going to do? Can you make it home?"

She looked around for help, but whoever had started down the alley had left.

"Come on," she urged him, helping him to his feet. "You can do it, Pete." When he was standing, she grabbed the flour sack with one hand and wrapped her other arm around Pete. "You can make it home. I know you can."

They stopped once, and Grace saw that the handkerchief was soaked through with blood. She pulled off her hat and gave it to Pete to use instead. While she waited for him to catch his breath, she glanced into the sack and saw that along with the bottles, all the eggs had broken, too. Bits of glass and egg yolk mixed in a sickening yellow goo with the bread that had fallen out of its paper wrapping.

There went supper, Grace thought as she set the bag down—and tomorrow's breakfast, too.

EVICTED

Getting Pete home to Mama was all Grace could think about as she struggled to help him walk up the sidewalk toward the apartments. Suddenly, though, a small cry pierced the frigid air, and she stopped to listen.

"Pete, do you hear that?" Grace asked, taking her arm from around her brother.

"I do," Pete said, his voice muffled by the hat pressed against his nose.

"Someone's crying," Grace said, her voice trailing off as she realized the sound came from one of her own little brothers.

Grace lifted a hand to cover her mouth as a nightmare unfolded. There on the sidewalk outside the apartments, Mama sat on her four-poster bed while Iggy and Owen sobbed into the folds of her skirt. Piled up around them were the rest of the family's belongings.

Blinking hard did nothing, Grace discovered. The nightmare only clarified. Under the falling snow, Mama clutched something white—her wedding dress—and rocked back and forth.

"I can't believe it," Pete whispered behind Grace. "They evicted us."

"Those men?" Grace asked.

Pete nodded. "They threw us out for not paying the rent."

Slowly, Grace approached. She saw that a floor lamp that had once cast its cozy light over the armchair in the living room now stood outside, its long electric cord trailing back toward the building as though pointing the way to where this crime had taken place. The sofa, with bureau drawers full of clothes stacked upon it, was dropped against the streetlight pole. The kitchen table had been left upside down beneath a pile of chairs. And nearby, other things—bedding, pots, toys, dishes—had been tossed into a heap, like so much junk, beside the road.

"How could they do this?" Grace asked.

"It's legal," Pete said. "All the landlord cares about is his money."

When he stumbled, Grace reached out to steady him.

"You'd better sit down," she told him, helping her brother to the curb. She found a blanket to put around Pete's shoulders. Then she pulled a quilt from off a coatrack where it had been tossed, shook the snow off, and draped it over her mother's head and shoulders.

"What happened, Mama?" she asked, kneeling in front of her and putting her arms around Iggy and Owen.

Owen stopped crying for the moment, but Mama didn't say anything. She just kept rocking back and forth, her sad, empty eyes fixed nowhere.

Looking around, Grace saw Grandma Rosa's carved

wooden clock, smashed, on the concrete and leaned over to pick up the tiny red-and-white bird that had cuckooed the hour for so many years. While her fingers closed around it, she saw the family's Victrola on its side, broken into two parts. Her eyes darted about to see if she could spot the records. Instead, Grace spied her cigar box, contents spilled, in a pile of sheets that included Mrs. Hewitt's unlaundered linens.

Would Mrs. Hewitt ever know what happened?

On her hands and knees, Grace hastily gathered her treasures before they were buried by snow: the hair ribbons and the oyster shell, the postcard of the Statue of Liberty, the pencil sketch of her beloved pet rabbit, the list. But where was the strawberry-shaped pincushion she kept in the box?

As she looked for it, she knew she would never in her life forget the indignity of having her mother's underwear on the ground for everyone to see, or the stinging pain of finding precious, framed family pictures strewn about like discarded candy wrappers.

She rescued a small painting of the Scottish Highlands that Grandmother McFarland had done, and the brass candle snuffer that used to sit on the fireplace mantel, and the cut-glass candy dish that had been a wedding gift to Mama, but then her hands were full, and she didn't know where to put it all.

Meanwhile, Pete sat on the curb, still holding Grace's hat against his bleeding nose, until Papa returned.

"Those unspeakable cowards!" Papa railed. "This was a gutless act! Coming here behind my back!" He walked around in a circle, pounding at the air with his fists and cursing, until finally, he went over and hollered at Pete. "Why don't you say something? What happened here?"

"Papa!" Grace cried, dropping everything in her hands and rushing to him. "Pete's hurt! Martin Jeeter beat him up!"

But Papa wasn't listening, and Mama wasn't any help at all. Grace began to cry. She ran to her mother. "Mama, please!" she begged, yanking the wedding dress out of Mama's hands so she would pay attention. "Do something!"

Mama stopped rocking. Her eyes slowly shifted to focus on Grace. "Go," she said simply. "Go and get Aunt Emma."

Grace threw down the wedding dress and ran. She ran as fast as she could. Even at intersections, or when the walk became slippery with snow, she barely slowed down. On and on she ran, driven by the horror of what had happened. She tried not to worry too much about what she would do if Aunt Emma was home alone. Aunt Emma was deaf, and Grace only knew how to finger spell the alphabet. She wasn't sure she could form enough letters fast enough to make her aunt understand. But there would be some way to tell her. Some paper in the house maybe. A pencil and paper so she could write.

When Uncle Stewart answered the door, Grace was so relieved, she burst out into tears and words at the same time. "Help! We've been evicted! Everything is on the street! Everything!"

Aunt Emma rushed to embrace Grace while Uncle Stewart signed and interpreted the bad news. Moaning, her aunt tightened her arms around Grace.

Uncle Stewart ran a hand through his hair, thinking. "I'll

get the suitcases in the attic." He signed to Aunt Emma and told Grace, "Grab the milk crates on the back porch."

After leaving their three small girls with a neighbor, they were ready. Uncle Stewart didn't have the car he drove for the rich family, so they walked back, a walk that seemed to take forever. Grace struggled to go fast, but the suitcases were bulky and bumped against her legs.

When they finally arrived, Grace was glad to see that Mama had come back to her senses and was gathering things to take. Owen dragged a broken chair toward the pile Mama had started, and even Iggy was trying to help by gathering up spoons and forks.

"Where's Pete?" Grace kept asking. But no one seemed to know.

"Get all the bedding you can," Uncle Stewart instructed. "I'm not sure I've got enough for us all."

Grace stuffed Mama's favorite flower vase into a satchel filled with clothes. She had already rescued her cigar box again, and Pete's small leather sack full of marbles. Dutifully, Grace draped two blankets over her shoulder, tucked her cigar box under one arm, and grabbed a bed pillow and her wooden hairbrush with her other free hand.

Another family's belongings were dumped on the sidewalk not far away, but no one seemed to care except for an old man, who stood holding an umbrella and silently staring at the pile.

Not a single neighbor came out to help. Grace wondered why. Were they scared? Of what?

Papa hoisted several thick quilts but left his fiddle in its case on the ground so he could grab one of the lanterns instead.

"What about Pete?" Grace asked Uncle Stewart. "He might have a broken nose. We can't leave without him."

"He knows where we are," Papa answered.

"I'm sure he'll be along," Uncle Stewart assured Grace.

It was starting to get dark. With tablecloths and extra sheets, Uncle Stewart covered the remaining furniture, but Grace heard Papa mutter that it would be a miracle if nothing was stolen overnight.

"Keep the faith," Uncle Stewart told Papa as they set off. "The Lord will provide." But the boys never stopped whimpering, and Grace worried. Not just about Pete but her mother, too, who never looked back and didn't say a word as they trudged up the sidewalk through the gathering snow.

A Temporary Measure

At Uncle Stewart's house, electric lights and warm radiator heat awaited them. And soon Aunt Emma filled the small quarters with the welcome smell of milk toast.

Grace helped by using wooden tongs to dip each slice of toast into a bowl of hot water. After the toast was moistened, she put it on a plate, and Aunt Emma ladled thickened warm milk over it. Mama opened two cans of corn and heated the contents in a pan on the stove.

Everyone was hungry, but as soon as they had finished saying grace, Papa pushed back his chair and stood up. "I can't eat," he said. "I'm going to look for Pete."

Aunt Emma hurriedly began to sign. Uncle Stewart nodded in agreement. "I'll go with you, Clement."

No one said much after they left. Even the little boys and Aunt Emma's three small daughters ate without a fuss. Afterward, Mama dabbed at her eyes with a handkerchief and went to lie down because of stomach pains.

Grace collected the dirty dishes from dinner and stood at the sink drying while Aunt Emma washed. She tried to imagine where Pete might have gone. To the church? To the road underpass, where hoboes hung out after they jumped off the trains coming into Washington?

Aunt Emma touched Grace on the shoulder and told her in sign, "No worry." But Grace saw how her aunt bit her bottom lip as she washed the dishes.

With both hands, Grace took each wet plate and moved the towel around its edges. What would her family do? she wondered. They couldn't possibly stay crowded in at Aunt Emma's for very long.

Owen tugged at Grace's skirt. "We want a pony ride," he told her.

"A pony ride?"

Owen nodded eagerly, his innocent face lighting up at the prospect of having Grace down on all fours, giving them rides around the kitchen table. Iggy and the cousins watched Grace, waiting for an answer, and she knew that none of them really understood what had happened that afternoon.

"Wait until I'm done," Grace told them.

After she had finished the dishes, Grace was true to her word. Then, when she didn't think her knees could take it anymore, Grace built a blanket fort behind the living-room couch and the kids crawled in excitedly.

Relieved, Grace went to sit on the floor beside Mama, who was stretched out on the couch. She waited there until Papa and Uncle Stewart returned, their arms full of snow-covered belongings, but without Pete.

Mama sat up. "You can't find him?"

Papa handed Mama her wedding dress. "Not a sign."

"He's a smart boy. We know he's found cover somewhere," Uncle Stewart tried to assure them.

Aunt Emma rushed to warm up supper and fix plates for the two men.

When they finished, Uncle Stewart ushered everyone back into the living room and tried to sound cheerful. "Let's listen to some radio, why don't we?" But only a scratchy snatch of music came through the boxy brown device. "I'll bet that's the Wakefield Song Birds," he kept saying.

"I think so," Mama agreed, but her voice was flat. Grace knew they were all just passing time, waiting for Pete to return.

Leaning in close, Uncle Stewart slowly adjusted the radio dial some more, capturing a few muffled lines from *The Chase and Sanborn Hour*; but the reception only got worse, probably because of the weather, and finally, he turned it off.

Owen and Iggy and their girl cousins still huddled in their fort, giggling.

Grace sat on the floor and hugged her knees. Why didn't Pete come home? she wondered. And what was going to happen to Mama's bed in the snow? And Papa's fiddle? Snow wouldn't be good for the strings or the wood. And what about the ceramic bowl she and Mama used to make cookies and bread. Did someone pick it up? The bowl made her think of the silver mixing spoons; she had stepped on one. She wished now she had picked it up and stuck it in her coat pocket. But then her thoughts came around to Pete again, and she knew that nothing really mattered except that Pete was safe.

Papa watched Mama staring at the front door, and a lump grew in the back of Grace's throat.

All at once Papa stood up. "I'm going back out to find him," he said.

Uncle Stewart pushed himself out of his chair.

"Can I go, too?" Grace asked.

Papa shook his head. "No. Stay and help Mama and Aunt Emma."

The rest of the evening dragged by slowly. When it was time to sleep, Grace's mother made a bed in the dining room and let Owen and Iggy curl up with her. The cousins—Violet, Virginia, and Vivian—slept, packed like sardines, on a pullout couch that took up most of the living room, so Grace folded a blanket and lay in the only other space available, the kitchen floor. She rolled up an old sweater to use as a cushion beneath her head. Then she took from her dress pocket the small painting of Scotland by Grandmother McFarland, put it in the cigar box with Pete's marbles, and held the box close to her when she lay down to sleep.

All night the hot-water radiator in the kitchen clanged and the kitchen faucet slowly dripped, making a tiny *plink* as each drop hit the tin sink. But they were oddly comforting sounds. Grace wouldn't have to haul buckets in the morning, and she didn't have to sleep with her coat on. If she could sleep at all. How could she sleep when all their things were being covered by snow? And with Pete still out there somewhere, cold and hungry and hurt?

Grace folded her hands. "Please, God, watch over Pete until Papa and Uncle Stewart can find him." She pressed her thumbs against her forehead and squeezed her eyes shut as she prayed, over and over, until she fell asleep.

In the middle of the night she was awakened by Iggy's crying.

"He's holding his ear," Mama said tiredly, signing at the same time to Aunt Emma.

Aunt Emma turned on a soft light by the stove and rummaged in the cupboards until she found some tea.

"Mint is fine," Mama said, pulling out a chair at the table. She sat, cradling Iggy awkwardly to one side of her huge belly. Then she signed with her free hand to Aunt Emma, asking aloud at the same time, "Do you have some bacon grease? Bacon grease, yes. We'll warm some up to put in his ear."

It was later, with grainy gray light seeping in around the curtains, when Grace was awakened again, by the sound of the door opening. She pushed off her blanket and jumped up when Pete hobbled in, supported by Papa and Uncle Stewart. Mama rushed to help him into a chair in the kitchen.

Everyone cringed at the sight of Pete's grossly swollen nose, bruised and caked with blood.

"I found him under a roadway bridge," Papa said. "Some tramps had a fire lit. Got his first taste of bootleg whiskey, I imagine."

At the mention of *bootleg*, Grace flashed a look at her father.

"God bless them," Mama said, putting an arm around Pete's shoulders. "They probably kept him alive."

Aunt Emma handed Mama a cloth she'd soaked in warm water, and Mama began, gingerly, to wipe off the dried blood from Pete's face. His nose had a big hump in the middle of it. "Hard to breathe," he mumbled, wincing at Mama's touch.

He was thirsty, too. Grace returned to the kitchen sink three times to refill his glass and helped him hold it steady while he drank.

But the worst thing about Pete was the way he shivered and how he couldn't catch his breath without starting to cough all over again. Pete was always coughing, but this time the cough made Aunt Emma nervous.

They moved Pete out of the kitchen then, onto a rug in the dining room, where he was covered with lots of blankets and left to sleep. Grace stood mute in the doorway, staring at her brother's flushed face, listening to his ragged breaths, and felt a chill, like a frozen rod, run through her.

At breakfast, there was work to be done. Grace helped her aunt by getting the children seated and handing out small bowls of grits. After everyone had eaten, the adults remained at the kitchen table, stirring cups of coffee. Grace hovered near the sink, waiting to hear what was going to happen, but Papa sent her away to watch the children and keep them quiet.

"Do as you're told," Mama said.

Reluctantly, Grace left the room. "Go fetch a book," she told three-year-old Vivian. "Find *The Tale of Two Bad Mice* and I'll read it to you."

The little book was Vivian's favorite. When she returned with it, Grace sat in the armchair with the children gathered around her. "'Once upon a time there was a very beautiful dolls' house,'" Grace began.

Out in the kitchen, Mama asked Papa, "Should you make another trip back, Clement, for a few more things?"

Grace softened her voice as she read so she could hear the adults talking. "'It was red brick with white windows.'"

"We needn't bother going back," Papa said. "What's worth saving is gone. We saw, Stewart and me. They've even taken the bedposts for firewood."

Mama made a small sound and must have started crying.

"Come on, *read!*" Vivian urged, pushing her elbow into Grace.

Grace held a finger to her lips. "Shhhhh!"

"What about your father in the country?" Uncle Stewart asked Mama. "Could he take you in?"

Grace's eyes grew large. Grampa Schmidt was ornery—and his house didn't have running water! You had to use a dark and scary outhouse that smelled to high heaven and had splinters in the seat.

"He's as bad off as we are," Mama said.

While she turned the book from side to side so the children could see the dolls' house, Grace peered through the kitchen doorway and saw Mama frowning. "Clement and my father go head-to-head on everything."

"What about Fritz? Your brother out in Ohio?" Uncle Stewart asked.

Mama looked down at the table.

"Fritz's wife, Min, has polio," Papa told them.

Uncle Stewart sighed and put a hand on the back of his neck. "I just thought he could use your help running the farm."

Mama shook her head.

"We couldn't possibly impose," Papa said.

The kitchen grew silent. Vivian turned a page in the book

and Grace read quickly, "'It belonged to two dolls called Lucinda and Jane.'"

"I wanna *see*. I can't *see*!" Virginia whined from her place at Grace's feet.

Grace handed her the book.

"Then there's no alternative," Uncle Stewart declared. Grace watched him put both his hands on the table. "Emma and I were talking last night. There's a children's emergency home, a mission run by the church, up near Kann's Department Store. You can leave the children there until you're back on your feet. At least until after the baby's come."

A mission? Grace frowned. What in tarnation was *that*?

Grace pushed herself out of the chair. "Show them the pictures," she told Virginia.

When she got to the kitchen doorway, Grace could see Mama's tired red eyes slowly filling with tears. Grace had known her family couldn't stay at Aunt Emma's. She and Uncle Stewart barely had enough room and food for themselves. But a mission?

"A temporary measure," Uncle Stewart assured them. "The children will have three square meals a day and a warm bed to sleep in."

"Are you sure? Will they take care of them?" Mama's voice quavered.

Aunt Emma tapped Mama's hands and signed to her.

"Yes, they are Christians," Uncle Stewart repeated so Papa understood.

Grace's stomach grew tight. What would this mission be like? How long would she have to stay? Even for Christmas?

Papa stood by the window and stroked his beard as he looked outside.

Uncle Stewart put a hand on Papa's shoulder. "Pete needs a hospital," he said. "It's obvious to all of us, Clement. The boy is terribly sick."

Papa covered his eyes. "A hospital," he mumbled. "God knows we don't have the money for that."

"The hospital at Thirteenth and Upshur will take him," Uncle Stewart said.

Grace stopped breathing. Thirteen was an unlucky number.

"They take the indigent. You don't need any money," Uncle Stewart explained. "And I suggest we do it right away. I've got Ornfield's car this morning. I say we pack up and take them immediately. Grace and the boys first. Then Pete to the hospital."

Papa turned to Mama. "I don't see that we have a choice, Ruth."

Mama shook her head and bit her bottom lip.

Grace felt the whole world freeze. Not just her breath but her hands, her heart. Inside, everything froze.

The rest happened fast. In a blur. A spinning top with pictures that became a solid color as it spun around.

"Grace, gather your things," Uncle Stewart told her.

There was not much to gather. Her coat, her cigar box.

"Good-bye, Pete," Grace whispered, kneeling on the floor beside him. His face was moist with fever, his eyelids were drowsy, and when he coughed into his hand, she thought she saw a spot of blood.

"Oh, Pete," she said.

He tried to smile.

Grace covered his limp, sweaty hand with her own.

"I have your marbles," she told him. "Do you want them in your pocket? For good luck?"

"No," he said weakly. "Keep them for me, will ya?"

"If you want," Grace said. "But promise me you'll get better."

Pete took a breath, but he was too tired to talk anymore.

In the kitchen, Mama hugged Grace, long and hard. "There isn't room in the car for everybody. I can't go with you," she said. "But you understand, don't you? This is just temporary. Until we get back on our feet. Then we'll be together again. The family."

Grace nodded against Mama's shoulder and tried hard not to cry. Not in front of Aunt Emma and Uncle Stewart and all her cousins, who were watching like little hawks. Mama finally let her go and pushed the loose hair out of Grace's face. "Watch out for Owen and Iggy. Keep an eye on them."

"I will," Grace assured her.

Uncle Stewart and Papa were waiting at the door. Grace pulled on her coat and scooped up the cigar box from her place by the stove. Then she returned to the dining-room doorway to wave one last time to Pete; but he had already closed his eyes.

CHILDREN LIKE US

The mission was a big brick battleship of a building that towered over the narrow sidewalk in a busy part of Washington, D.C. Grace felt very small walking up its front steps and dreaded what was coming. She imagined the mission to be like a cold, cavernous church, where she would have to sit stoically, praying all day with her hands folded and her back straight, on a hard, narrow bench.

Inside the front doors, however, Grace was relieved to feel warmth. The smell of coffee and oatmeal filled the air, too, and people of all ages came and went busily in the small vestibule. Papa took off his cap and moved Grace, Iggy, and Owen off to one side.

"Are you here for the party?" a man asked brightly.

Grace thought the man looked like a pirate because he had a patch over one eye and several days' growth of beard. He didn't look like someone Grace could trust, and she started to feel afraid again.

"We're . . . uh . . . we're here to see the director, Mrs.

Claiborne," Papa stammered, slowly turning the tweed cap in his hands.

"Oh, but you have to stay for the party, too. The First Lady is coming this morning! She's going to distribute Christmas gifts to the children."

Papa seemed flustered. "Do you know where we can find Mrs. Claiborne?"

The man said he would check.

"The First Lady?" Grace tugged on her father's coat sleeve. "Who's that?"

"Are we going to a party?" Owen asked excitedly.

"The First Lady is the president's wife, Mrs. Hoover. And no—*no*," Papa added sternly, "we're not going to any party."

The pirate man beckoned to Papa.

"Be right back," Papa said. "I probably need to sign some papers."

While they waited, Grace took off her mittens and stuffed them in her pocket, where her fingers discovered the cuckoo bird from Grandma Rosa's clock. She had forgotten about the little bird. Grace put it in the cigar box and placed the box and all their coats on an empty chair. Then she sat, pulling Iggy onto her lap.

"Come here, Owen," she said, patting the folding chair beside her.

Owen struggled so hard to get up onto the chair that Grace had to grab the back of his overalls to help him up.

"Are we staying here?" he asked.

"Shhhhh," Grace warned because his voice seemed loud. "Yes, we're staying for a while."

"Where Mama?" Iggy asked.

"Back at Aunt Emma's," Grace said. "She's taking care of Pete because he's sick. "

Owen looked up at Iggy, who sat on Grace's lap. "Pete is sick. He needs a cloth on him's head."

Grace nodded. "Yes. Mama put a facecloth on his forehead because of his fever."

Owen put a hand on his own forehead and then asked, "Who is here?"

Grace looked at him. "Do you mean in this building?"

The little boy nodded.

"Other children. Children like us," Grace tried to explain.

"Like *us?*" Owen frowned.

"Just kids, Owen," Grace said impatiently. "Kids like us who need a place to stay. That's all."

"Oh." Owen sat back in the chair, apparently satisfied with the answer.

When their father returned, a tall, attractive woman wearing stylish clothes accompanied him. Papa had a hard time looking at them and had to clear his throat a couple of times before he told them, "This here is Mrs. Claiborne."

The woman smiled kindly. She shook Grace's hand and reached out for Owen's, but he pulled his back, and then so did Iggy.

"Boys!" Papa tried to snap the word, but his voice had lost its edge.

Mrs. Claiborne waved her hand. "That's okay," she said sweetly. "We'll get to be friends later, I'm sure."

Papa cleared his throat. "Mrs. Claiborne here says the mission will provide for you."

"You're not staying, Papa?" Owen asked. "Kids like us are here."

Papa shook his head. "No. I can't stay, Owen. But as soon as Mama and I have another place, we'll come back and fetch you."

He reached out then. Grace eased her grip on Iggy and squeezed her father's rough fingertips.

"Keep an eye on the boys for us, Grace," he told her.

Grace swallowed hard. She didn't want to cry in front of the lady in fashionable clothes. Briefly, she met Papa's red-rimmed eyes, and nodded.

Papa tousled the hair on Iggy's head and touched Owen's cheek. "Be a big boy," he said.

Then Papa left, putting his cap back on as he went and walking faster and faster. He never once looked back. Grace watched through watery eyes until he was gone. She could still hear his heavy boots on the wooden floor out in the hallway when Mrs. Claiborne started talking.

"This is Miss Mabel," Mrs. Claiborne said, introducing a thin, disheveled woman who flashed them a quick smile, showing her crooked teeth. "She'll be taking care of you."

Grace didn't think Miss Mabel seemed too happy about her new chore.

"We're all very, very busy this morning," Miss Mabel told them in a voice that seemed made for scolding. "We've got the president's wife coming today. So let's get you cleaned up and let's do it quickly."

Upon standing, Grace had the odd sensation of feeling completely drained of all emotion. She watched numbly as

Owen and Iggy left eagerly with Mrs. Claiborne, who had promised them a peppermint stick if they were good.

"This way!" Miss Mabel barked.

Grace followed the woman upstairs to a large bathroom. The room was every bit as big as Aunt Emma's kitchen, with a window up high and electric lights in the ceiling. There was a flush toilet, too, with a chain to pull, and big, square, black and white tiles on the floor.

Miss Mabel opened a closet and laid a clean white towel over the back of a nearby chair. She unwrapped a big bar of yellow soap and set it in a wire basket on the side of the large claw-foot tub. Then she leaned over to stick a rubber plug in the drain and turned on the faucets. Hot water gushed out, and steam rose above the tub like a cloud.

"What did you say your name was?" Miss Mabel asked.

Grace was still marveling at the faucets, wondering if the bath and the clean towel and the big bar of soap might possibly be for her.

"Your *name*, child," Miss Mabel repeated.

"Ah—Grace McFarland, ma'am."

"Grace. Is your head itchy, Grace?"

"No, ma'am," Grace replied. "It might be dirty, though. I haven't had a bath for some time."

Miss Mabel came over to examine Grace's scalp more closely, but Grace didn't like the feel of Miss Mabel's bony fingers poking around on her head and pulled away.

"Well, I don't see any lice," Miss Mabel said, putting her hands on her hips and regarding Grace suspiciously.

"Certainly not!" Grace exclaimed. She knew what lice were;

the kids at school called them cooties. She'd picked up the wretched insects once last year. Mama even had to comb kerosene through her hair to get rid of them.

"Still," Miss Mabel said, "if you're going to be here awhile, we need to be sure you're good and clean."

"But I'm not going to be here long!" Grace told her.

Miss Mabel narrowed her eyes. "You're not one of those, are you?"

"One of *those*?" Grace asked.

"One of those *impudent* children."

Grace didn't know what *impudent* meant, but it sure didn't sound like a compliment. She dropped her eyes, afraid suddenly that word would get back to Mama and Papa that she'd misbehaved. "I only meant I wasn't going to be here long, Miss Mabel. Just a couple days. Until my folks find a new place."

Miss Mabel snorted and turned around to stop the bathwater. "Go ahead. Get in. And undo that braid so we can wash your hair," she ordered.

After Miss Mabel left, Grace took off her clothes and undid the braid. With her long hair rippling down her back, she eagerly stepped into the warm bath and sat, sliding back against the end of the tub until the water came up to her chin, covering her, like a cozy blanket.

Suddenly, Miss Mabel strode back in with a pot in one hand and some clothes in the other.

Grace grabbed the edges of the tub and pulled herself up, then quickly crossed her arms over her chest.

"We'll get this ole mop of yours good and clean!" Miss

Mabel sounded amused. Pushing up her sleeves, she scooped water into the pot and dumped it over Grace's head.

Gasping, Grace covered her eyes with her hands. She kept them there, too, the whole time Miss Mabel scrubbed Grace's scalp with the yellow soap.

"There! That should do it!" Miss Mabel wiped her hands on a towel and pointed to the clothes on a nearby chair. "After you dry off, you can get dressed."

Grace wiped at her eyes.

"Go ahead! Soap yourself up now and don't be long about it."

Obediently, Grace picked up the soap and began rubbing it on the washcloth.

"In the meanwhile I'll take care of all this junk," Miss Mabel said as she bent over to scoop up Grace's boots and clothes from the floor.

"Please! Not that," Grace pleaded.

Miss Mabel held up the cigar box. "This?"

"Yes, ma'am," Grace said politely.

"No food in here, is there?" Miss Mabel frowned. "Nothing to draw mice?"

Grace shook her head. "Just some pictures," she said. "And a few things from home."

Miss Mabel grunted, then slid the box under the chair and left.

Grace held her breath until she heard the door latch. Only when she was sure Miss Mabel was not going to intrude again did Grace allow herself to relax and enjoy the bath. She scrubbed and rescrubbed several times before climbing out of the tub.

When she was dry, she picked up the clothes left on the chair. They were hand-me-downs, faded and soft with use. But they were far better than anything Grace had had for a very long time. She kept checking, but the black woolen stockings were without a single hole. The brown-and-white Oxford shoes were supported by thick rubber soles. And the dress . . . Golly, Grace thought, she would never forget holding that dress up the first time. It was dark green with a full skirt, fancy white smocking across the bodice, and puffy sleeves, each capped by a single brass button. Grace couldn't wait to put it on.

Quickly, she pulled on underwear and stockings and a white slip with ruffles on the bottom. Then, finally, the dress, which settled over her slender little body with room to spare. Even after Miss Mabel returned and tied the dress's bow snug behind Grace's waist, the garment hung off Grace's shoulders and fell well below her knees. Still, Grace thought the green dress was beautiful. She ran her hands over it, across the bumpy white smocking, down the smooth skirt. She plucked at the sleeves and then looked down at her feet. Even if the shoes did pinch her toes, they were shoes of which to be very proud.

"Hmmmpf." Miss Mabel crossed her arms and grunted. "You're a right pretty little girl when you're cleaned up."

Embarrassed, Grace cast her eyes down.

"You won't have no trouble finding someone," Miss Mabel said.

Grace jerked her head up. "What did you say?"

"I said you won't have no trouble," Miss Mabel repeated. "Somebody will take you home."

"But I don't want to go home with anybody," Grace replied.

Miss Mabel pointed at her. "You listen, young lady. You're not the one giving orders around here. If someone offers to take you home, you go, you hear? Now turn around!" she ordered. She began running the comb through Grace's long hair, hit a tangle right away, and yanked so hard that Grace grimaced and had to hold onto the back of a chair for balance.

"Miss Mabel," Grace began timidly, "I can't go home with anyone. I have to watch my brothers."

But Miss Mabel ignored her. "Everyone helps around here," she rattled on. "You'll be making beds and working in the kitchen."

Grace bit her lip. She would just refuse, then. No one could *make* her go. Could they?

"Here. I give up." Miss Mabel thrust the comb into Grace's hands. "Follow me. You can finish that hair upstairs."

Grabbing her cigar box, Grace followed Miss Mabel and wondered where they were going. The new shoes felt heavy on her feet, but she liked their snug, slippery feel and the solid sound they made on the steps.

On the third floor, Miss Mabel led Grace into a cold room and pointed to an iron double-sized bed beneath a window. "This is where you'll sleep."

Grace noticed there were four other beds in the room, too.

"Three girls to a bed," Miss Mabel announced curtly as she opened a corner cupboard and set a flannel nightgown, a toothbrush, and some socks on the bed. "These are yours. You can put your stuff in the bottom drawer of that bureau there. The other drawers belong to the other girls. You're *not* to go into them."

Miss Mabel marched out the door, still giving orders. "We rise at seven!"

Grace set her box in the bottom drawer and pushed it in. But she hesitated before leaving the room to follow Miss Mabel. So there were other girls, she was thinking as she stared into the room. Girls like her. One of them might become a friend. Maybe they would be like sisters. Sisters who talked and giggled and called cranky ole Miss Mabel names behind her back.

It might even be fun, she thought; but the idea was fleeting because underneath, Miss Mabel's words—"somebody will take you home"—had stirred up a tiny ripple of fear that kept returning now, like the beginning of a bad stomachache.

Seconds on Soup

I want to go home!" Owen cried, running up to Grace and throwing his arms around her legs.

"Owen, careful—you'll knock me down!" Grace loosened his hands and knelt to give him a hug, just as Iggy rushed up behind them both. "Wan Mama. Wan Mama," he whimpered. And Grace put an arm around him, too.

Both of the boys had been given baths and wore fresh clothes. Grace could smell and feel their clean, wet hair against her cheeks.

It was lunchtime, and all the children at the mission were filing into the dining room.

"When are we going home?" Owen asked. "I don't like it here with children like us."

Grace looked into his wide, frightened eyes and realized that Owen still didn't understand that there was no home to go back to. Should she try to explain it? How? She squeezed her brother's hand. "Did you have a nice bath, Owen?" she asked instead. "Doesn't it feel *good* to be clean?"

Owen shook his head and scowled. "Don't like the bath."

Grace tried to coax a smile from him. "Come on. We just got here! You haven't given it a chance."

She glanced around at the children, many of them, like her, wearing clothes that were either too big or too small. Some were laughing and talking, others stood quietly, sucking a thumb or with hands thrust deep into overall pockets. One little boy had lips chapped so badly that they were cracked and caked with dried blood.

"We can't go home yet," Grace told Owen. "We have to stay."

Iggy entwined his little fingers with those on Grace's left hand and would not let go, not even when it was time to sit down.

As they settled themselves at two long tables, Grace let Iggy crawl onto her lap. She looked up and down the rows of faces and counted twenty-six children altogether, boys and girls both, of ages that ranged from about two to fourteen or older.

"Let us bow our heads in prayer," said the pirate man. Grace folded her hands over Iggy's and heard her stomach turn with hunger. She coughed a little to cover the noise.

"We give thanks, O Lord, for this daily bread and all that You have provided," the man continued. Grace peeked to see what indeed the Lord had provided and spied from the corner of her eye a large platter piled high with chunks of corn bread. She closed her eyes again quickly, wondering if each of them would be allowed an entire piece of corn bread or if the pieces would be cut in half. Maybe even quarters because they were so big.

When the prayer ended, Grace's eyes flicked open to see

two pitchers of milk being set down on the table. Grace hadn't had fresh milk for weeks. She reached eagerly for her cup, but everyone else was standing up, bowl in hand, and forming a line at one side of the dining room.

"Pick up your bowls and follow me," she told the boys.

The line moved quickly. One by one, each of the children walked up to a window between the dining room and the kitchen, where they placed their bowls on a small wooden counter and waited for a generous ladle full of navy-bean soup. When her bowl was filled, Grace saw tiny pieces of ham floating in it, and her mouth began to water.

As soon as they were seated, the children began eating, their spoons busily clanking against the soup bowls. Corn bread was passed around and milk poured. Owen reached eagerly for his milk while Iggy took up his corn bread in both hands, eating hungrily and littering his lap with crumbs. The soup was thin, but it was hot. When Grace paused to take a drink of cold milk, she closed her eyes in pleasure and finished the entire cup without stopping.

"More?" a young woman asked, standing by with the pitcher in hand.

Grace nodded and watched in disbelief as her cup was refilled.

There were seconds on soup for those who wanted it, even another half piece of corn bread. Grace waited, and watched in awe, when her cup was refilled with milk for the third time.

As stomachs filled, the children relaxed and began to talk.

A girl sitting across from Grace introduced herself as Sarah. "Did you just get here?" she asked, leaning forward. She seemed a little bit older than Grace, twelve maybe, and had a heap of freckles sprinkled on her face and carrot-colored hair that had been chopped off, just above her shoulders, as straight as a broom bottom.

"This morning," Grace told her. "With two of my brothers. We're only here for a couple days. Until my parents find a new apartment."

Sarah smiled at her. "Two brothers?"

"Actually three," Grace said.

"You're lucky," Sarah said. "I don't have a brother *or* a sister."

Grace had never considered herself lucky to have so many brothers, only unlucky because she didn't have a sister.

"What's your name?" Sarah asked.

Grace finished licking the last crumbs of corn bread off her fingers. "Grace. My name's Grace."

Another girl across the table overheard. "Hey! My name's Millie," she called out. "And this here's Constance," she added, indicating with her thumb the girl beside her. "Miss Mabel said y'all was sleepin' in our bed now."

A smile slowly spread across Grace's face. These were the girls, she realized. Her new sisters: Millie with two blond pigtails, and Constance with a head full of curly brown hair.

Millie flipped a braid back over her shoulder. "So, Grace. Y'all better not have no cooties."

"No sir! And you'd better not snore neither!" added Constance, talking with her mouth full. "Or we'll kick you out. Won't we, Millie?"

It was not a joke. Millie was frowning at Grace. "You bet! We'll boot your butt right out of bed!"

Overhearing this, some of the children at the table giggled. Grace was flabbergasted.

"You're *not* being very nice," Sarah scolded them.

"Mind your own beeswax, Sarah!" Constance retorted.

"Is there a problem here?" Miss Mabel asked, suddenly appearing at the head of the table.

Sarah looked at Grace, but Grace shook her head and swallowed hard.

Millie wiped her mouth with the back of her hand and went back to eating. Miss Mabel left.

"Don't mind them, Grace," Sarah said loud enough for the other two girls to hear. "They're two little twits who make trouble for everyone."

Grace felt her stomach sinking. She finished eating without looking up from her bowl.

After lunch the girls carried around the new dolls they had received in bags of gifts from Mrs. Hoover. Grace guessed that she had missed the morning party while she was having a bath. She was disappointed she hadn't gotten to see someone as important as the president's wife. And she was sad because she had lost the doll she once had. She had carefully packed the doll in a box with her clothes the first time her family moved. But the box had been lost, and no one ever found it.

"This place is really not so bad once you're used to it," Sarah told Grace as they walked around the tables together, setting down forks and spoons for dinner.

"How long have you been here?" Grace asked.

As Sarah placed the next spoon, Grace noticed how the girl's fingernails had been chewed down to the quick.

"Eight months tomorrow," Sarah replied.

Grace's mouth dropped, but Sarah didn't see because she was glancing at the clock above the kitchen door. "I need to get ready," Sarah said. "I'm going home with a family this afternoon."

"Going *home*?" Grace asked.

"Not *my* home," Sarah quickly explained. "Another family has invited me for dinner. People do that sometimes. Invite one of us home for a spell, for supper and the evening, maybe. I don't even *think* about getting adopted anymore. Most people, they only want little kids."

She leaned forward to whisper to Grace. "I'm hoping, since there are only a couple days until Christmas, that I'll be invited to stay for the holiday. I sure don't want to be *here* on Christmas morning."

"No," Grace readily agreed. No one would want to be here on Christmas morning, she thought. But behind the thought her mind was spinning. Did Sarah say some kids *wanted* to be adopted? If so, that meant there were orphans at the mission. And it sounded as though Sarah was one of them.

"I didn't mean it won't be fun here on Christmas!" Sarah said suddenly. "They're putting on a party for all the kids. I heard them talk about it. And for dinner they'll have a turkey and everything. It'll be wonderful! You'll see!"

Grace forced a fake smile. "Christmas doesn't matter to me, Sarah," she said, even though it wasn't true.

Sarah seemed surprised.

"But I love turkey," Grace said, clutching the forks in her hand. "So I'll look forward to dinner. Whatever you do, don't feel sorry for me."

Sarah regarded her uncertainly and then glanced at the clock again. "Well, I guess I need to go. Look, Grace, I usually help in the kitchen after lunch. Maybe you could take my place today. The cook's name is Mrs. Potts. I guess you won't forget where *she* works, right? Mrs. *Potts?*"

Grace grinned slightly at the joke.

Mrs. Potts was fat and had a round, red face dotted with beads of sweat. She was kind, however, and greeted Grace with a compliment. "Such pretty, long hair," she said.

A mound of potatoes waited to be peeled.

Grace picked up the paring knife and went right to work. As she did, she thought about Mama and Papa. And about poor Pete so sick. But then Constance and Millie barged into her thoughts, their voices repeating in her head: *Better not have no cooties . . . We'll boot your butt right out of bed. . . .* If Pete were here he'd tell Grace not to take those insults sitting down. Next time, Grace might just pop stupid little Constance on the nose and yank on Millie's braids until she cried. She could cuss them out, too, the way Mary Orlinsky back at the apartments would. She could call them "little turds" and "sniveling little brats."

The peeling stopped. Grace didn't want to cuss out the other girls. She wanted to be their friend.

"You're awfully quiet," Mrs. Potts said as she cut pieces of meat for stew. "I know it's hard being away at Christmastime. But you're not alone."

Grace turned the potato in her hand and resumed peeling.

"I see you got some presents from the First Lady today," Mrs. Potts said. "She's grand, isn't she?"

The potato slipped out of Grace's hands and hit the floor with a thud. "I didn't see Mrs. Hoover," she replied, reaching down to pick up the vegetable. "And I didn't get any presents."

Mrs. Potts put down her butcher knife. "Is that the truth?" she asked, coming around the butcher block.

"Yes," Grace told her.

"Well, we'll see about that!" Mrs. Potts declared, wiping her hands on her apron. She left the kitchen and returned with a large bag tied at the top with green and red ribbons. "Just one left!" she announced cheerily. "And I put *your* name on it."

Stunned, Grace put down her knife and reached for the bag. But Mrs. Potts pulled it back. "No, no, no! Not until you're done. Then you may take the bag and open it."

Never had Grace peeled so many potatoes so quickly. When she was finished, Mrs. Potts handed her the bag and grinned, her fat cheeks doubling in size. "Enjoy your doll!"

Not knowing where else to go, Grace raced up the stairs to the third-floor bedroom she shared. She was disappointed to see Millie and Constance and some of the other girls there. But when they saw the bag, they gathered around, eagerly watching as Grace struggled to get the ribbons off.

Finally, the bow gave way and the bag was opened. At first Grace was confused, because inside was a large red fire truck and a small-sized firefighter's hat. She pulled them out and looked for the doll, but there was just some candy, a blue yo-yo, and a metal badge that said FIRE CHIEF.

For a moment there was silence. Then one of the girls said quietly, "You got a boy's bag."

Constance and Millie snickered and covered their mouths.

Grace wanted to run away and cry. Instead, she swallowed hard and put the fire truck back in the bag. "My little brothers will love this truck," she said, replacing the firefighter's hat, too, and then rolling the top of the bag closed.

No one spoke. Calmly, Grace set the bag by the bureau and left the room. Only when she got as far as the stairs did she break into a run, descending as fast as she could.

At the bottom of the three flights of stairs was an open door and more steps leading to the basement. Grace rushed halfway down, then stopped, scared to go farther because it was so dark. She sat, holding her arms, feeling how hot and flushed with embarrassment her face was and wishing she could be anywhere but here.

When something moved in the darkness, Grace sucked in her breath. Should she run back upstairs? No, she decided; she would rather be shivering, inches away from a rat, than upstairs with people who were mean. All Grace wanted was to go home.

Even if there was no home to go to.

And in that moment, Grace understood something that she would never forget: Home wasn't just a building or an apartment with a roof and beds and chairs inside. Home was with her family, wherever they were.

Her eyes softened as she remembered the night when they had to sleep in the church. The bank had said they couldn't live in their house anymore. All their things were packed up, but they didn't have an apartment yet; and Uncle Stewart was sick with influenza, so they couldn't stay at his house. There was nowhere else to go. When they knocked on the Reverend Saunders's door at the parsonage, Papa couldn't lift his head, he was so ashamed.

The reverend was in his bathrobe and wore fuzzy slippers on his feet. "Come in, come in," he told them, beckoning with a turn of his hand. He gave them fruitcake on paper napkins and buttermilk in tall glasses. He found blankets and led them with a lit candle into the empty church, where Mama made up beds on the pews. The church was cold, but moonlight glowed on the organ pipes, and Grace felt safe.

She hoped it didn't offend the Lord, sleeping in church like that—especially the way Papa snored. But in the morning, when the first long rays of sun streamed through the tall, stained-glass windows above the choir loft, Grace pushed herself up and saw how a rainbow fell silently, a secret blessing, across the faces of her sleeping family.

Do for Themselves

Grace! Get up here! It's time to eat!" Miss Mabel's voice boomed from the doorway above, startling Grace. But after two hours of sitting on the hard stairs, hugging her own thin arms and breathing the musty, dank air, she was not sorry to be found. By then Grace was hungry again, and a supper of beef stew, biscuits, and cold milk tasted mighty good, even if the meat was stringy with fat and the biscuits hard.

When they finished eating, the younger children were called away for a bedtime story. But before they left, Grace gave Owen and Iggy each a hug and told them about the fire truck.

"For *us?*" Owen asked, thumping a finger on little Iggy and pointing to himself.

Grace smiled. "I'll give it to you tomorrow. You go on to bed now."

Owen took Iggy's hand.

"Sleep tight so the bedbugs don't bite," Grace called softly as the two boys walked away together.

In the bedroom with the five iron beds it was cold. The girls undressed quickly, peeling off layers of stockings, slips, and dresses. Grace dug out her flannel nightgown but then stood silently, holding the garment close to her chest, because she had never undressed in front of strangers.

Contance stared at her. "What are *you* waiting for?" she asked.

Grace dropped her eyes but didn't answer. Then, when the girls lined up at the bathroom door to take turns sprinkling baking soda from a large container onto their toothbrushes, Grace stood at the back of the line, waiting to be last. By the time she returned with her teeth brushed and her clothes neatly folded, all the other girls were in bed, most of them snuggled in with their new dolls.

Grace set her shoes on the floor and pulled open her drawer. She put her clothes inside, then lifted the lid of the cigar box and took out Pete's bag of marbles so she would have something to hold, too.

Clutching the marbles, she walked over to the bed, where Millie and Constance had already claimed the edges, leaving only a narrow space in the middle. Grace would have to crawl over one of the girls and squeeze into it.

A knot grew in her stomach. Her only other choice was to curl up on the cold, hard floor, without a blanket to keep her warm or a pillow beneath her head. But would it be better?

"Hortense! Get back in your room!" Miss Mabel's harsh voice crackled down the hall. A door closed. Her footsteps came closer.

Pressing her lips together hard and squeezing the bag of marbles in her hand, Grace crawled over Millie's feet, trying her best not to touch them. Millie pulled her feet in and yanked the blanket taut across her shoulder. Constance did the same, securing the blanket so tightly that when Grace pulled on it, it wouldn't budge and she couldn't get under.

"Grace! In bed!" Miss Mabel ordered as she strode toward the bed. Constance let go of the covers and Miss Mabel whipped them down.

Grace crawled between the two girls and lay on her back, her toes curled and the marbles tight in her hands.

"I don't want any trouble from you," Miss Mabel warned. Then she whipped the blankets up over the girls, flicked off the light, and left.

For a moment there was silence. Grace didn't dare move. She knew if a fight started, she was outnumbered. So even her breathing was carefully controlled. In on the count of three, out on the count of four. Grace imagined she must look like Grandma Rosa, the way she was laid out in her coffin, all stiff and straight, and the thought of it made her face contort.

Suddenly, a funny little noise erupted from one end of the room. Someone with the hiccups? The sound punctuated the silence again. One of the girls was crying? When Millie beside her started sniffling, Grace realized that the entire room had slowly filled with tiny, muffled sobs.

Grace knew that she could have sat up in bed and called them all a bunch of big babies, just to get back at Millie and Constance for being mean. But she didn't because she knew that they were just girls, not unlike herself, misplaced through no fault of their own. If she had let herself, Grace could easily have cried with them. More than anything, she wished she could be with Mama and Papa, even if it meant sleeping on Aunt Emma's kitchen floor and listening to the faucet drip all night.

Gradually, the crying stopped and was replaced by the quiet, rhythmic sounds of breathing. Grace lay silently with her eyes wide open, afraid to go to sleep for fear her leg would relax and roll into Constance, or that her elbow would brush against Millie's back.

She wondered if Owen and Iggy were snug in a bed together. And she wondered what it was like for Pete, in the hospital.

It was sometime later when Grace heard the door hinges squeak and saw yellow light from the hallway spill inside the room. A small figure appeared. A girl. A girl holding a large, awkward arm full of bedding.

Grace sat up. "Sarah!" she called softly, recognizing the girl.

"That you, Grace?" Sarah whispered back.

Carefully, Grace crawled down to the end of the bed and knelt at the iron foot railing. "How come you're back?"

Sarah tiptoed over to her. "I sneezed too much."

"You *sneezed*?" Grace asked.

Sadly, Sarah nodded. "I was allergic to their dog."

"Gosh," Grace sympathized. "What happened to your bed here?"

"Miss Mabel had to give it to a new girl," Sarah said.

"Oh," Grace said. "So where are you going to sleep now?"

"On the floor. Miss Mabel gave me some blankets."

Grace glanced at the floor. "I'll sleep down there, too, if you want," she offered. "Can I share your blankets?"

Sarah seemed surprised. "Sure."

Grace moved quietly so as not to wake Constance and Millie. She was glad to be free of her coffin position in the bed. Even with a quilt beneath them, the floor was hard. But lying beside Sarah, Grace found it was a lot easier to breathe.

"Grace?" Sarah whispered in the dark. "Are you still awake?"

"Yes."

"I just wondered," Sarah said. "Are you afraid of anything? I mean, *really* afraid?"

Grace tapped her fingers on her mouth. She was afraid of a lot of things. Mad dogs and polio came to mind. Also hunger, and being cold. But Grace didn't want to confide all these things to Sarah, a girl she'd just met.

"I'm definitely afraid of rats," Grace told her, selecting one fear instead of all of them. "I hate rats."

Sarah didn't respond. In fact, she was quiet for such a long time Grace figured that was the end of the conversation. Odd, she thought, finally closing her own eyes to sleep.

"I'm afraid of trains," Sarah whispered. "My parents died on a train."

Grace's eyes popped open.

"It went off the tracks. Out in Colorado—in the mountains. We were going out there to live, only I wasn't with them because I was finishing school. I was to take the train later, with Grandmother."

Grace lay still, not knowing what to say.

"We couldn't have a funeral," Sarah said. "It was too expensive. My parents were buried in a little town close to the accident. When my grandmother broke her hip, they sent me here, to the mission."

Grace turned to Sarah, but in the darkness she couldn't see the girl's face.

"At first," Sarah went on, "I told everybody it was just for a couple days. Until my grandmother got home from a trip. But then, when she never came, everybody knew I made up the story. No one got mad, though, because everyone does it when they first get here."

Grace frowned. Did Sarah think that Grace had made up a story about her parents coming back in a couple days?

"Sarah," she began carefully, "do you know *any* kids from the mission who went home again with their parents?"

"One," Sarah said. "There was a boy named Danny who left with his mother. He was here almost as long as me."

Grace sighed with relief.

After a moment Sarah rolled over, pulling the blanket off Grace.

Poor Sarah, Grace thought. All alone in the world. Without parents. How could God let that happen to a nice girl like Sarah?

Maybe being nice didn't make a difference, Grace pondered. It was not the first time she had examined this thought because lots of nice people she knew had suffered for no reason. People like those in her own family. Maybe God just couldn't reach down this far to help, she thought. Maybe people just had to do for themselves while they lived out their lives.

Letting her breath out slowly, Grace turned on her side and curled up tight, with her back against Sarah's. Then she reached down to pull the bottom of her nightgown over her cold feet and used her own arms to keep herself warm.

GUARDIAN ANGELS

In the morning, a loud bell clanged sharply, splintering Grace's dream and making her heart race. It had been a restless night, but Grace managed to get a portion of the blanket back. Now, as Sarah sat up, the blanket was pulled off again and Grace shivered from the cold.

"Time to get up," Sarah murmured sleepily. "We need to help with breakfast."

"You slept on the floor?" Constance, a bemused expression on her face, hovered over Grace from the bed above.

"I prefer it down here," Grace replied, looking Constance in the eye.

But the truth was that the floor felt like ice. Grace pulled on her stockings first, then the slip and the green dress. She started raking her fingers through her long, tangled hair, but Sarah, who did the bow on Grace's dress, said there wasn't time to braid it just now, or even to find the comb.

In the kitchen, a tall pot of oatmeal was already bubbling. Grace stuck her head in the warm steam and enjoyed the good smell. When the oatmeal was ready, Sarah gave her a ladle and told her to spoon the cereal into twenty-six bowls. When she finished, Grace filled twenty-six tin cups with milk, each of which she placed carefully on the counter between the kitchen and the dining room.

When Owen and Iggy came to the window with the other children, they saw Grace in the kitchen, and Iggy began to cry.

"My brothers," Grace told Sarah.

Mrs. Potts overheard. "Go ahead and sit with them, dear."

Grace was grateful that Mrs. Potts was so kind. She wiped off her hands and went to the boys. Iggy wrapped his arms around her and wouldn't let go.

"He cried all night," Owen said, looking tired, and a little bewildered.

Iggy rubbed his eyes and murmurred, "Wan Mama."

"Come on," Grace said, taking their hands. "Let's have some nice hot oatmeal."

"They're cute," Sarah said to Grace as she sat down across the table.

Grace didn't have time to reply because suddenly, Miss Mabel appeared at the table and everyone stopped talking.

"Sarah, my dear," Miss Mabel said in a surprisingly pleasant voice. "I want you to sleep in the nursery the next couple of nights. Some of the little ones are having trouble sleeping. I need an older child in there to keep things calm."

"Yes, ma'am," Sarah replied.

"And *you*, Grace!" Miss Mabel's voice took on a sharp edge. "Let's cut that hair today! It's a disgrace! You can't work in the kitchen with your hair all over the place!"

Grace was horrified. "But I'm going to braid it, Miss Mabel!"

SAVING GRACE

Miss Mabel just grunted and moved on down the line to yell at a little boy for not blowing his nose.

Upstairs after breakfast, Sarah found a comb and tried to help Grace get the tangles out of her hair. "Don't worry," Sarah kept saying, "Miss Mabel's always yelling. It doesn't mean she'll follow through."

Still, Grace chewed on her lip nervously as Sarah made a single braid with Grace's hair and tied the end with half a shoelace.

Even with Sarah's reassurance and a neat new braid, Grace carried the worry with her all day. At any moment, she thought, Miss Mabel might appear with a heavy pair of shears and make her stand for the cutting—or worse, scalp her from behind. What would Mama say? Grace had never had her hair cut. Never! It wasn't Miss Mabel's right to do it!

Oh, help, Grace thought. She needed to get out of there. All afternoon, while Grace struggled through hours of tedious work, sweeping the floors, stocking soup cans in the pantry, scraping dozens of carrots, she had tried to figure out how she could escape.

She would wait until after dinner, she decided, when the children were supposed to line up in the lobby and sing Christmas carols. No one would miss her then with so much going on. All she needed was her coat and the cigar box from the drawer upstairs. Once she was outside, she could find her way to Aunt Emma's. Mama would understand. Mama and Aunt Emma would both understand about cruel Constance and mean old Millie and Miss Mabel. They wouldn't make her return—in fact, they would rush right back to rescue Iggy and Owen, too! Especially when they found out they might be taken home by other people.

After dinner, while Grace and Sarah swept the dining room and wiped down the two long tables, a deliveryman came in the back door with snow-dusted bottles of milk. "Getting mighty messy out there," he commented. The bottles clinked as he set them down. He rubbed his hands to get them warm. "Must be four inches on the ground and more to come, they say."

Grace didn't have any boots. How could she walk through all that snow? Would she recognize the streets if they were covered up?

As children filled the lobby, lining up to sing Christmas carols that evening, Grace realized the escape plan was no good. And the thought of sleeping stiffly in between Constance and Millie—and the fear that Miss Mabel would cut off her hair—made her stomach turn into one gigantic knot.

Nearby, an older man sat down at a tall upright piano that had been rolled into the lobby. As he played the opening notes to "Silent Night," a flood of Christmas memories washed over Grace, squeezing her chest. Once again she saw Santa Iggy and the train made from Spam cans. She saw Papa's big grin as he weighed a bag of pistachio nuts in his hand, and heard Mama's delighted squeal as she opened a box of colorful ribbon candy.

How Grace yearned to be sitting beside Mama in the big chair that had been left out on the sidewalk. Was someone else sitting in that chair now? Had someone brushed off the snow and carted it home in a wheelbarrow? Was there a girl Grace's age sitting in that chair now, with a mother who was reading stories and rubbing her back?

The ache for Mama was bad. Grace could feel the warm tears pooling in her eyes. She struggled to keep her head from dropping, knowing that Miss Mabel would scold. Thank goodness Owen and Iggy were off in another room making paper Christmas ornaments. She didn't want them to see her crying.

A small crowd of people had been invited to hear the children sing. Grace watched as two well-dressed ladies joined the audience. One of them looked like a movie star with her jaunty hat and fur coat. Grace blinked and, with the back of her hand, wiped the tears from her eyes. She wondered what the ladies were doing here and was horrified to suddenly see one of them pointing at her. Not a moment later, Miss Mabel was at the end of Grace's row, motioning for her to come forward.

Grace panicked. Had it been obvious that she was crying? Her bottom lip trembled. What kind of trouble was she in now?

"Grace, come here, dear," Miss Mabel instructed.

Dear? Miss Mabel was calling her *dear?* Grace wiped off her cheeks a second time as she made her way out of the line and down the steps.

Miss Mabel took her hand. "I want you to meet someone." Grace was scared and bit her lip.

"This is Miss Elizabeth Hammond," Miss Mabel said. "And this is her sister, Miss Louise."

"How do you do?" Grace replied shyly.

"How do *you* do?" one of them replied. Their smiles seemed so genuine. Grace couldn't imagine why they would want to punish a little girl for crying.

"For the last two years the Hammonds have helped us out," Miss Mabel told Grace in a firm voice. "They wondered if this year you would like to be the one to join them at their home for the Christmas holiday. I have assured them you are quite healthy *and* that you are well behaved."

Grace looked at her uncertainly.

Miss Mabel seemed impatient. "It's okay," she insisted. "Your parents know another family may take you in for a while. Some of the children are fortunate that way."

"But my brothers," Grace said, beginning to shake her head. "I'm supposed to take care of them."

Miss Mabel cracked a phony smile. "Ah, you're such a good sister. But do you know that tomorrow morning they will be going to the Fox Theater to watch cartoons and have a big Christmas party? I don't think they're going to have time to even *think* about missing you, Grace."

Grace knew it was rude to drop open her mouth. But even she had never been to a theater to see cartoons. "Are they going to see Mickey Mouse?"

The ladies chuckled.

"Probably," Miss Mabel said. "He's all the rage, you know."

Maybe, if Iggy and Owen were going to see Mickey Mouse in a moving-picture theater . . . then maybe a couple days away wouldn't be a big deal.

"Run upstairs, Grace, and get your things," Miss Mabel directed. "Quickly!"

When Grace returned, the two ladies were waiting by the door with an empty satchel for Grace's clothes. And suddenly it hit her what was happening.

Unbelievable. Just wait'll she told Pete, Grace thought, beaming now—absolutely beaming with confidence—that Mary Orlinsky's fortune-teller was right after all. Grace had been sent not one but *two* guardian angels!

THE HAMMONDS' HOUSE

Grace was so caught up in the magic of her escape that she didn't care if her shoes filled with snow. It was possible, she thought, that at any moment Miss Elizabeth and Miss Louise might sprout wings and carry her off into the snowy sky. Instead, the three of them tromped two more blocks through the deepening snow and caught the trolley.

The trolley was crowded with people bundled up against the cold. Many of the passengers clutched shopping bags, and some of the women wore Christmas corsages with snow-frosted greenery and tiny colored balls. As the trolley jerked and started to move, a man stood so that Grace and the Hammond sisters could sit together. Grace was squeezed in so tightly between the two women, she could smell their flowery perfume and peppermint breath.

"Don't worry about a thing now. We'll get your feet dry as soon as we're home," Miss Elizabeth said. Grace couldn't help staring at Miss Elizabeth—she was so glamorous with her bright red lipstick and curly dark eyelashes.

"Are you hungry?" Miss Louise asked. When the trolley

swayed, Miss Louise grabbed onto the seat back in front of them with a small gloved hand. She wasn't as flashy as Miss Elizabeth, but with her short, wavy hair and soft brown eyes, Miss Louise was still just as pretty, Grace thought.

"Are you, dear?" Miss Louise repeated sweetly. "Are you hungry?"

Grace nodded shyly. She was always hungry.

"Good!" Miss Louise said. "We've got a beef roast at home tonight. On Christmas we'll stuff a turkey and have three kinds of pie."

Miss Elizabeth adjusted her hat and winked at Grace. "Say, what kind of pie do you like?"

Looking from one to the other, Grace felt her eyes widen. "Pie? Any kind," she said dreamily. "Especially apple."

Miss Louise smiled at her. "That's my favorite, too!"

As the trolley clanged and lurched its noisy way up Connecticut Avenue, Miss Elizabeth, who insisted Grace call her Miss Betsy instead, and Miss Louise chatted nonstop about the boardinghouse their family ran and all the "interesting characters" Grace was going to meet.

Grace must have looked confused.

"A boardinghouse, Grace, is where people rent rooms—and get a meal or two," Miss Louise explained. "Most of our boarders rent by the week, although we do have a few who come and go."

"Oh, and I do wish that some would go!" Miss Betsy rolled her eyes.

Miss Louise waved a hand at her sister. "Everyone is *very* nice."

"In fact, there's a girl just your age. And another—our younger sister—who's a little older than you," Miss Betsy said.

"She'll love Johnny, won't she, Betsy? Johnny loves to play checkers. He's my husband, Grace."

Her *husband*? Grace didn't think Miss Louise looked old enough to have a husband.

The trolley stopped in front of the zoo. "Our stop!" Miss Louise announced cheerily.

Grace could hardly believe it. "You live near the zoo?"

"Right across the street," Miss Betsy said.

Grace looked back to the zoo entrance. This was like a story, she thought, something out of a book!

Miss Louise took her hand. "We'll go tomorrow if you like. One of the elephants has a darling baby."

The Hammonds' boardinghouse on Connecticut Avenue looked like a regular house from the outside. Inside it did, too—except that it overflowed with Christmas. As soon as they entered, Grace caught sight of the tall, fragrant Christmas tree standing in the living room beside the piano. The tree glittered with dozens of shining ornaments, and beneath it a mound of presents brushed the lowest branches. Even in happier days Grace's family had never had a tree as grand as this one, and certainly not so many presents.

"Come in, come in," an older woman beckoned. Behind her, pine boughs with red bows festooned the white banister and cascaded, like waves, down the stairwell.

The big front door closed with a heavy thud behind them.

"Mother, this is Grace," Miss Betsy announced. "Grace McFarland."

"Ah, welcome to you, Grace," Mrs. Hammond said, taking both of Grace's hands in her own. "Come in near the fire and warm up. We're so glad you've come to spend the holiday with us."

"Thank you, ma'am," Grace said as she was led beside a crackling fire in a huge brick fireplace in the living room.

Other people arrived and more introductions were made, but it was hard to keep everyone straight. The young girl her age was Esterbelle. That was easy to remember. And Esterbelle's mother was Mrs. Scarlotti. Then the pudgy, bald gentleman with the three-piece suit was Swede. And Johnny was the handsome young man with black hair who winked at her and then kissed Miss Louise on the cheek.

"Maybe Grace would like to freshen up a bit," Miss Betsy suggested.

"Of course." Miss Louise led Grace upstairs and down a long, carpeted hallway. "Our family sleeps on the second floor," she explained. "The boarders are up on the third floor. You'll sleep here, in Betsy's room. Johnny and I are right next door. Our sister, Joanna, is across the hall, and Mother and Father have the room there, next to hers."

Miss Betsy slept in a big brass bed. Grace was told she would sleep on the rollaway near the bedroom fireplace. She saw that a fresh towel and washcloth had already been laid out on the red afghan that covered the small bed. It looked cozy, Grace thought, and would be so much better than squeezing in between two spiteful girls, or sleeping alone on a hard floor.

"You can wash up before dinner if you like," Miss Louise said. "Oh, and here are your things." She set the satchel on Grace's bed. "There's a bathroom just down the hall, the first door on the right. Take your time. When you're ready, come on down. We'll be having dinner in just a few minutes."

She closed the door, and for a moment Grace was alone again. She looked around at the fine room Miss Betsy had: the mahogany dressing table, the thick, patterned carpet on the floor, the fireplace and its mantel adorned with framed family photographs.

Stepping up close to the mantel, Grace examined the pictures and was able to pick out Misses Louise and Betsy standing beside a piano. There was a picture of Johnny and Miss Louise, in her wedding dress. And in another photograph Miss Louise and Johnny were holding a baby.

At the dressing table Grace opened a box of body powder to smell it, then touched the silver-handled brush that Miss Betsy used and peered into an opened jewelry box filled with shiny earrings and necklaces. "Wow," Grace mouthed as she touched a sparkling, star-shaped diamond brooch. She picked it up to feel its weight and tilted it side to side in the palm of her hand. At the pawnshop she and Pete could get ten dollars—maybe even *more*, a lot more!—for a piece like this.

Grace set the pin back in the jewelry box and went to find the bathroom, which, she discovered, was even more marvelous than the one at the mission. A clean white tub; stacks of thick, colorful towels; shelves filled with lotion, soap, and powder. Grace glanced at herself in the mirror above the sink and was disappointed to see an ugly smudge of dirt on her chin and that her braid had loosened, leaving long strands of hair to dangle down one side of her face. She licked a finger and rubbed at the spot on her chin, then tucked the loose hairs behind one ear and washed her hands.

Downstairs, Grace was seated at the table between Miss Louise and Miss Betsy. As soon as Mr. Hammond finished the blessing, Grace watched with wonder as the two ladies on either side of her piled her plate high with slices of roast beef, mashed potatoes with gravy, string beans, and applesauce. Three times Grace reached into the bread basket for a warm baking-powder biscuit, two of which she split open and slathered with butter. The third one went quietly into her lap, where she folded it inside her napkin and secretly slipped it into the side pocket of her dress.

While Grace ate, conversation flowed around her. Gradually, she connected more names and faces. Mr. Hammond sat at the head of the table and said Grace was "cute as a button." Two friends of Miss Betsy were guests, not boarders, who sang with her in a group called Three Maids and a Mike. "The *mike* is short for *microphone,* not a man," Miss Louise explained. "People are always thinking someone is missing when they show up."

"I still can't believe we got that spot," Betsy was saying. "Pure luck!"

Miss Louise leaned toward Grace. "She's going to sing on the radio next Sunday. We're all very excited."

"How's the writing going?" Mrs. Hammond asked Mr. Parker, a serious-looking, gray-haired gentleman.

"Quite well," Mr. Parker replied. "I wrote almost an entire chapter today."

From the end of the table, Mr. Hammond raised his eyebrows at Grace. "I'll bet you didn't know you'd be staying with a famous singer *and* a published author, did you?"

"No, sir," Grace answered in awe.

"Grace, may I have the biscuits?" Esterbelle asked.

Esterbelle, sitting across from Grace, had green eyes and dark hair she wore in long, tidy ringlets that were pulled back and tied with a red-and-white striped bow. The bow matched her dress.

"Thank you," Esterbelle said, accepting the basket with fingers adorned with red nail polish. Self-conciously, Grace peered down at her own hands and saw to her dismay that despite yesterday's bath, dark crescents of dirt lay under her ragged fingernails.

"Do you have a talent?" Esterbelle asked as she buttered her biscuit. "Do you sing or dance? Do you play the piano?"

Grace desperately wished she could say yes to one of those things.

"I'm taking tap-dance lessons," Esterbelle went on without even giving Grace a chance to answer. "I'm getting quite good, too, aren't I, Mother?"

Mrs. Scarlotti grinned.

Golly, Grace thought. There was nothing special like tap dancing that she could do. There wasn't money for lessons like that. And Papa never did get around to teaching her how to play the fiddle. But was there anything *special* she could do? Grace rummaged through her mind. She could whistle "Dixie" all the way through—and she was pretty darn good at ringer and boxies, because Pete taught her how to knuckle down and flick the marble with a little backspin. Biting her lip, Grace glanced at Esterbelle and knew instantly that neither of these things was special enough.

"I'm learning to knit!" she suddenly remembered, brightening. "My mother is teaching me."

"Knit?" Giggling, Esterbelle glanced around the table. "Did you hear that? Grace is learning to knit!"

"I think it's wonderful that Grace is learning to knit," Mrs. Scarlotti said rather firmly. And Grace realized that Esterbelle had been making fun of her.

Grace looked back to her plate, her appetite suddenly gone, and wondered if Esterbelle was going to pick on her the way Millie and Constance had. Why? Why wasn't it just as easy to be nice instead of cruel?

"Joanna!" Mrs. Hammond exclaimed. "You must be feeling better!"

Grace looked up to see a young girl enter the room and stand at the head of the table. She was older than Grace—Pete's age maybe—with a slight build, skin as pale as chalk, and honey-colored hair cut into a cute bob. There was nothing at all striking about her appearance, and yet the shy, kind look in her soft blue eyes caught and held Grace in midglance.

"You haven't met this member of the family," Mr. Hammond said, reaching out to put an arm around the girl's waist. "This is Joanna, our youngest. She hasn't been feeling well today."

Miss Betsy whispered to Grace, "Joanna is deaf."

Esterbelle overheard. "Yes, you need to look directly at her when you speak," she instructed loudly, and rather self-rightously, Grace thought.

"Joanna," Mrs. Hammond said, pointing to her plate. "Do you want to eat?"

The girl shook her head.

Meanwhile, Grace stood up quietly and, turning toward Joanna, lifted her right hand to her forehead and made a saluting motion, the sign her deaf aunt Emma used to say *hello.* Then she spelled out with her fingers, which moved quickly because she knew the letters well, "My name is Grace."

Everyone was watching, and from the corner of her eye, Grace saw with satisfaction that Esterbelle's mouth had dropped open. Joanna, meanwhile, smiled for the first time since she had come to the table and enthusiastically made a sweeping motion toward herself, the sign Grace knew to be *welcome.*

"Grace! You know how to sign!" Miss Louise exclaimed.

Grace wrinkled her nose. "Not much. But I do know how to finger spell. My aunt Emma is deaf. It's how I've always talked to her."

"She finger spells?" Miss Louise asked. "She spells out everything?"

"Oh no. She uses sign language, too," Grace said. "She went to a special school to learn it. You should see her talk with Mama. Their hands go so fast you can't believe they're having a conversation. They tell jokes and everything!"

"Your mother is deaf, too?" Miss Louise asked.

Grace shook her head. "No, Mama learned sign language

from Aunt Emma so they could talk to each other. They're sisters."

Miss Betsy leaned forward to join in the conversation. "A special school, you said. Do you mean your aunt went to a school for the deaf?"

"Yes." Grace nodded. "She wanted to go to college, too. To Gallaudet College for the deaf. It's right near where we used to live. But there wasn't enough money to send Aunt Emma—or Mama—to college. Aunt Emma worked at the college, though, before my little cousins were born. She was a cook. She took us to see a play there once. It was all in sign language, but even I understood some of it."

Miss Betsy seemed amazed. "Did you hear that, Father? A college where the *deaf* perform plays?"

Mr. Hammond stared over his glasses at her. "Betsy," he said sternly, "you know perfectly well how I feel about school for Joanna. Her place is at *home*, with *us*."

Miss Louise and Miss Betsy exchanged a look Grace didn't understand. Mrs. Hammond reached for her water glass. And Joanna stuck out her bottom lip and wriggled out of her father's grasp.

"Oh, come on," Mr. Hammond complained. "Let's not spoil Grace's first evening here with a family argument." He picked up his fork and knife and resumed, rather vigorously, cutting his meat.

"No, we mustn't spoil Grace's visit," Mrs. Hammond agreed. "Tell us, dear, what can we do for you this holiday to make it special? A trip to one of the museums maybe?"

"Or would you like to see a film?" Miss Betsy asked.

Grace's eyes lit up. "A film? I ain't never been to one!"

Esterbelle snorted.

A pause. Grace knew right away she'd used bad grammar. It slipped in at the worst times! She frowned at Esterbelle for being so rude and quickly corrected herself. "I mean that I have never been to one, Miss Betsy."

"Well, you name it," said Miss Louise. "Where would you like to go?"

Grace glanced from Miss Louise to Miss Betsy with their eager smiles and then looked at Joanna, who had come closer to stand behind her mother. Behind all their fresh, bright faces, Grace couldn't help but see the dark, shadowy images of her own family: Iggy's little hand scrunched around his ear, Owen searching for her at the mission, Pete hunched and coughing. . . .

"Where would I like to go?" Grace repeated the question slowly.

"Anywhere," Miss Louise prompted.

A movie. A museum. A candy store . . .

They were waiting for her to answer.

Grace turned to Miss Louise. "Then I would like to go see my brother," she said. "In the hospital."

Slipping Away

Silence settled around the table.

"Your brother," Miss Betsy repeated gently. "We didn't know you had another brother, Grace. Why is he in the hospital?"

"He's sick," Grace said. "Very sick."

Grace could tell she had disappointed them with her answer. But of course—why would they want to go to a hospital and see a sick person? Especially someone they didn't know? Grace panicked; she didn't want to displease them. If they weren't happy, they might send her back to the mission.

Joanna had pulled up a chair and sat with her eyes glued on Grace.

The air felt brittle. Grace scanned the waiting faces. "I'm sorry," she apologized hurriedly, "we don't none of us have to go to the hospital! We could go to the film instead—really! That's what I really want to do!"

But Miss Louise was shaking her head. "No, no, that's okay."

Johnny put his finger up in the air. "No reason we can't do

both!" He grinned at Grace. "We can visit your brother—then head on to a film! I know Laurel and Hardy are at the Palace."

"Or that play at the National—*Rebecca of Sunnybrook Farm*," Miss Louise suggested. "Either one sounds grand. What do you say, Grace?"

She nodded slightly, but she wasn't sure. Did they mean it?

"It's all settled, then!" Johnny reached over to pat Grace's hand. "One day after Christmas. We'll make a day of it."

Dessert was arriving. Dainty glass dishes of vanilla ice cream covered with chocolate sauce. Grace hadn't had anything this special to eat since a slice of hummingbird cake at the church picnic last August. The tension in the room seemed to have disappeared. Grace sighed with relief and dug into her cool, sweet dessert.

When she had finished, Grace automatically stood to help clear the dishes. It had always been her job at home.

"Why, Grace, how nice," Miss Betsy said.

"*I'll* help, too!" Esterbelle volunteered.

"Well, well!" Mrs. Scarlotti exclaimed. "This is a first!"

Grace didn't miss the dirty look Esterbelle cast her mother.

As she scooped up dinner plates and serving bowls, Grace was surprised at how much food was left.

"I see you really like those biscuits," Esterbelle said to Grace in the kitchen.

"I did. They were delicious," Grace said.

"Are you sure you wouldn't like another before I put them away?"

Grace put a handful of silverware into the sink and turned to look at Esterbelle, who glanced at Grace's pocket. Grace felt her cheeks grow warm. "Thank you . . . but I think I've had enough." She turned to leave.

"And if you expect to stay here, Grace," Esterbelle warned, "I wouldn't be showing off with any more of that sign language."

Grace swung around.

"No." Esterbelle lifted her chin and shook her head. "I wouldn't. They're trying to teach Joanna how to read lips. Mr. Hammond says she'll get along better in the hearing world that way. I heard him say so. And I'll bet if he saw you using sign language all the time, he'd send you right back to that mission."

With that arrogant pronouncement, Esterbelle brushed past Grace with her nose in the air and returned to the dining room.

Stunned, Grace stood, holding the back of a kitchen chair, and stared after the door that had swung shut behind Esterbelle's bouncing curls. Grace did not want to be a problem at the Hammonds' house. And she surely did not want to be sent back to the mission. Just thinking about the place made her stomach knot up.

As she turned back to the plates and platters heaped with leftover food, Grace's eyes blurred. The supper had been wonderful and the Hammonds were very nice people. But why did she have to be anywhere but with her own family? Did Mama and Papa have enough to eat tonight? She reached out to touch the cold, hard mound of mashed potatoes in front of her and felt guilty because her stomach was so full.

What she ought to do, she thought, is march right back into

the dining room and ask if they could take the leftovers to Aunt Emma's house. *I know when we opened the corn the other night, Aunt Emma's shelf was practically empty. . . .*

But would they think that was rude? What was Miss Mabel's word for it? *Impudent?*

Grace pushed through the swinging door and went to stand at Miss Louise's shoulder.

"Yes, dear?" Miss Louise asked.

"The leftover food," Grace began, finding that the words caught in her throat. "I—I just wondered . . ." An iron bed flashed into her mind. And a floor as cold as ice. "Is there anything else I can do to help clean up?"

After dinner everyone moved to the living room, where Miss Betsy played the piano and Mr. Hammond set up two card tables in front of the fireplace. Johnny rolled up his sleeves. "Grace, Esterbelle, Joanna"—he knocked on the table to get Joanna's attention—"how about a game of gin rummy?" He held up the cards, then a candy bar as he spoke to Joanna. "I've got a brand-new candy bar for the winner."

"A *Mounds* bar? Never heard of it." Miss Louise playfully swiped the candy from Johnny's hand and read the wrapper. "Chocolate-covered coconut."

As full as she was, Grace wanted that candy bar. She couldn't remember the last time she'd even had a *piece* of a candy bar. She sat down with the two other girls and picked up her cards one by one as they were dealt.

Mr. Hammond, meanwhile, talked with the author, Mr. Parker, about a new book Mr. Parker was reading. "*Tobacco*

Road," Mr. Parker said. "It's about those poor tenant farmers in the south. A real eye-opener, I'd say."

"A pity the way some people have to live," Mr. Hammond commented. "I knew a man back in West Virginia who was so desperately hungry, he and his family were living off wild greens, things they could pick in the fields."

Grace couldn't help overhearing. The Hammonds would be embarrassed, she thought, to know how she and Pete stole things because their family was desperately hungry, too. They'd cringe to know how Mama dried out and reused her tea bags. And no doubt they'd take her right back to the mission in a heartbeat if they knew Papa brewed bootleg liquor— even if it was to make money for food.

Mr. Parker removed the pipe from his mouth again. "The government has *got* to step in to help these people! And I don't mean charity. I'm talking about an honest day's pay for an honest day's work."

"Absolutely," Mr. Hammond agreed. "I think we're all waiting with baited breath to see what Roosevelt's going to do."

Over her fan of cards, Grace flashed her eyes at the two men. "Mr. Roosevelt is going to help my father get a job," she blurted out.

Everyone chuckled.

"Well!" Mr. Hammond exclaimed. "I'm glad to see we've got another Democrat in the house!"

Mrs. Scarlotti, who sat by the fireplace doing needlepoint, grunted. "Those Democrats will be the ruin of this country, you just wait and see."

When the card game was over, Johnny held up his arms in victory, then divided the candy bar into three pieces for the girls. Grace savored the sweet taste in her mouth and wished there was a way to save a piece for Pete.

Afterward, Miss Louise taught Grace how to play "Chopsticks" on the piano. Grace caught on right away and picked out the notes, over and over, with her two index fingers while Miss Louise played the bottom chords.

"I think we've got a young musician here," Miss Betsy declared. "And I must say it's good to see you back at the piano, Louise."

"It is," Mrs. Hammond agreed. "Really, dear. You should start playing again."

Miss Louise blushed. And Grace wondered why anyone who had a piano as nice as this one wouldn't be playing on it every day.

After one more round of "Chopsticks," Miss Louise said everyone surely had had enough. Laughing, the two of them turned around on the piano bench and dropped their hands in their laps.

Johnny clapped. "Good show!" he exclaimed, leaning back in the armchair where he sat. He stretched his long legs and put his hands behind his head. "Say, I was just wondering, Grace, about when we go see your brother. There are several hospitals in Washington. Which one's he in?"

Grace remembered only too well. "The one on Thirteenth Street," she replied.

"Thirteenth?" Mr. Hammond overheard and turned in his chair.

"I hope it's not bad luck," Grace said. All along she'd had a bad feeling about it.

Mr. Hammond seemed concerned. "Do you mean Thirteenth and Upshur?" he asked. "The hospital there?"

Grace nodded because that sounded right. "I think so. Uncle Stewart said it wouldn't cost Papa any money if Pete went there."

Miss Louise put a hand on her chest. "But that's the Tuber-culosis Hospital, Grace."

Johnny brought his arms down and sat up. "Your brother has consumption?"

Grace shrugged. No one had ever told her what was wrong with Pete. Consumption? All she knew about consumption was that the Fergusons' baby had it. It went to a special hospi-tal and never came home.

Miss Louise touched her hand. "Grace, we can't go to the Tuberculosis Hospital. TB—consumption—it's contagious. They're afraid people will catch it. Do you understand, dear? No one can visit."

Grace knew she couldn't cry. Not in front of all those people in the Hammonds' living room. It's a good thing she was prac-ticed at keeping things bottled up inside. Pete had taught her this. "Crying doesn't get you anywhere," he always said. But later that night, alone in Miss Betsy's room, Grace *did* let go. For a long time she cried quietly into the hands she cupped over her mouth.

She wondered if Mama knew that Pete had consumption. Did someone tell her? She was always making Pete sit in the steam. She worried about him so much. Mama. Grace wished she could be with Mama right then. It made her mad that some people had all the food and clothes they wanted and some people didn't. Even though they were good people, too!

"Why?" Grace asked angrily. *"It's not fair!"* And in the heat of her anger Grace did a bad thing. She opened Miss Betsy's jewelry box on the dressing table and took the star-shaped diamond brooch. She didn't even bother looking at it again, just put it in the cigar box and shoved the box under her bed. Mama deserved to have a pin like that, she told herself. And if Mama didn't want it, then she could sell it and have lots of money for food.

Sure, Grace knew it wasn't Miss Betsy's fault that Pete was so sick and Mama didn't have all the things the Hammonds did. She hit the button on the wall that turned out the light. But life wasn't fair, *was* it? Miss Betsy's family could buy another pin someday. They could probably buy anything they wanted! With the heel of her hand, Grace wiped the stupid tears off her cheeks.

The smooth, clean sheets on her little rollaway bed smelled like fresh flowers. It had been months since Grace had slept on real sheets. But she was not in the mood to relish the luxury. Her pillowcase, wonderful as it smelled, was already damp from her tears. More came, too, when she realized she had never said good-bye to Owen and Iggy. She had never explained to them why she was leaving. And she had not given them the fire truck.

Grace didn't think she'd ever get to sleep. But when she did, finally, she dreamed about the neighbor's house that caught fire on Bel Alton Street years ago. Even though she was little when the fire happened—six maybe—the memory remained poignant. She could still smell the acrid smoke and see the orange flames turning night into day.

The fire had started in the middle of the night. "Come see, Grace!" Pete had called to her. Grace pulled a coat on over her nightgown. The boots she wore—hand-me-downs from her older brother—were way too big for her feet and kept slipping off as she ran down the snowy street in the dark.

A crowd had gathered. Still catching their breath, Grace and Pete had stood with the others that night and watched as their neighbor's house caved in on itself with a violent implosion that whipped up the flames into a gigantic fireball. "Praise God!" everyone kept repeating, because the family and all seven kids were safe.

The next day, Grace and Pete had returned to snoop around. The family, they were told, had already been taken in by relatives out in the mountains of Garrett County. But stepping through the soggy, smoldering backyard, they discovered a black-and-white rabbit that had been left behind in a cage. Papa said they couldn't afford to have a pet. But Mama said it was okay to bring it home. She said somebody had to take care of it. Its hutch was all smashed in, but Pete fixed it. And Grace named the rabbit Patches.

For two whole years she lavished love on that rabbit, stroking his ears, hand-feeding it blades of grass and flakes of oatmeal, until the day she found the hutch door open and the animal gone. For days Grace cried, even as she went door-to-door asking if anyone had seen her black-and-white bunny.

Grace had always wondered how Papa could let her cry like that. He knew all along where it was. . . .

Suddenly, Grace sat up, holding a hand over her thumping heart. In the darkness across the room, Miss Betsy snored softly in her bed, and down the hall someone closed a door. Grace gripped the edge of the bed until she remembered where she was.

Slowly, she lay back down, pulling the covers back up, close, beneath her chin. But the dream, the memory, haunted her. And Grace couldn't shake the feeling that something precious, something important, was slipping away from her again.

THE SMELL OF CINNAMON

In the kitchen the next morning, Grace leaned forward to finish the last of her bacon and eggs and reached for a third cinnamon roll, immediately stuffing a huge sugary bite into her mouth.

Miss Louise chuckled. "Grace! You don't have to eat so fast! Slow down—you'll enjoy it more."

Grace put a hand in front of her mouth, embarrassed. She hadn't meant to be such a pig.

Miss Louise smiled kindly at her.

Grace took a smaller bite of the roll and watched, amazed, as Miss Louise poured real cream into her coffee.

It didn't seem real, Grace thought. Did she really wake up in a comfortable bed with a wool bathrobe at her feet? A warm radiator clanking in the corner of her room? The smell of the cinnamon wafting upstairs?

And then there was Miss Louise in the kitchen waiting for her. Miss Louise, who looked like a picture smack out of the *Ladies' Home Journal*, Grace thought. She was so pretty in her green silk dress and shiny pearl earrings. Everything about her seemed perfect: the way her short hair rippled with a fashionable wave; her hands, each long, dainty finger ending in a perfect half-moon of clean white fingernail. Grace couldn't help but remember with a twinge how, in winter, Mama's hands got so chapped that the knuckles cracked open and bled.

"I thought we'd do some shopping today," Miss Louise said. "Everyone else has gone to work, but I've got the whole week off."

Surprised, Grace looked up. "You work, Miss Louise?"

"Yes." She nodded. "Downtown, in a government office. Typing letters, filing papers. That sort of thing. It doesn't sound very exciting, but I like it. The people are nice, the money helps—and it does get my mind off things."

Grace used her finger to wipe up some of the gooey cinnamon sugar from her plate and wondered why Miss Louise had to get her mind off things.

Miss Louise sipped her coffee. "Anyway, I thought we'd get you some clothes today."

Grace nearly choked on the lump of roll in her throat. "Me? Get me some clothes?"

Miss Louise grinned at Grace's disbelief. "It will be our gift," she explained, reaching over to touch Grace's hand. "Because we know what it's like to be wanting."

Wanting? Nothing about the Hammonds looked as though they were wanting, Grace thought.

"You may find it hard to believe," Miss Louise went on, "but three years ago, we nearly lost everything we had. Father owned a general store in West Virginia then, and when times got hard and people couldn't afford to buy much, we went out of business. It's why we came to Washington. To start over."

Miss Louise picked up her spoon to stir her coffee again. "Believe me, we all had to pitch in to make it work. Betsy and I changed beds and swept floors. We chopped vegetables and made the salads every night. We washed the dishes. We took care of Joanna, too. She was just getting over pneumonia when we moved."

Grace recalled the picture on the mantel. "Was she just a baby then?"

"Oh, no." Miss Louise shook her head. "Joanna was your age when we came to Washington."

"Oh. I just wondered," Grace said, "because there was a picture of you and Mr. Johnny with a baby. I thought maybe it was Joanna." Grace took another bite of the roll and eyed the pan, wondering if she dared take a fourth. She didn't notice right away that Miss Louise had grown quiet.

"No," Miss Louise said softly. "That would have been my own little girl in the picture. . . . She passed away."

Grace stopped eating.

"She was five months old," Miss Louise said, her voice changing.

For a moment Grace worried that Miss Louise was going to start crying.

"And so we all moved here—to start over!" Miss Louise said quickly. "It was hard at first. Very hard indeed. Mother cooked all day and half the night. Father and Johnny ran the business side and did all the maintenance. Every chair that broke, every drawer knob that needed to be replaced, they did it all."

Grace knew she was talking fast so she wouldn't get sad again.

"After that first year, though, business *did* get better," Miss Louise continued. "We were lucky. Mother and Father still run the boardinghouse, but we were able to hire some help for making beds and doing most of the cleaning and cooking. Then Johnny, Betsy, and I were able to get the kinds of jobs we really wanted. Betsy with her singing, and Johnny—he works in a bank now and goes to law school at night."

She paused. "So you see, Grace, we do know what it's like to be wanting. And at Christmastime we like to give back a little."

Grace was still thinking about Miss Louise's baby. Losing that baby was probably why Miss Louise worked in the office, to get her mind off things.

Just then a bell rang at the back kitchen door, accompanied by a loud clunking sound.

"That'll be the iceman," Mrs. Hammond said, coming through the swinging door into the kitchen.

"In the nick of time, too." Miss Louise stood and pushed chairs aside to make a path through the kitchen. "What's left has just about melted."

A surge of cold air blew in with the iceman, who used tongs to carry and set a large block of ice in the icebox.

"When you're finished, you can go get dressed," Miss Louise told Grace.

Grace watched the iceman leave, then popped the rest of the roll into her mouth and set her dirty dishes in the sink.

Upstairs, she listened to the *tap, tap, tap* of Mr. Parker's typewriter in the room above hers as she made her bed, pulling the sheets and blankets taut and carefully tucking in the afghan around the edges. She washed her face, scrubbed her fingernails until they were clean, and put on the green dress again.

As she smoothed out the skirt, she felt in her pocket the biscuit she had saved from last night's dinner. The biscuit was hard, she discovered, unfolding the napkin. But it didn't matter. She had a feeling she would not need to snack on cold biscuits during the night here. But just in case, Grace rewrapped the biscuit and pushed it into a corner of her cigar box.

"Do you need help, Grace? With your hair?" Miss Louise called upstairs.

Grace put the box back under her bed and jumped up to take a look in the mirror. "Yes, please!" she called back.

Miss Louise's hands were not as sure of themselves as Mama's, but they were gentle. Grace told Miss Louise she was pleased with the two braids, knowing it would have been rude to ask her to undo them and make the one braid, like Mama's, that she preferred. She checked herself again in the mirror and this time noticed that Joanna was in the hallway, watching.

"Will Joanna come with us?" Grace asked.

"Oh no," Miss Louise replied. "She doesn't go out much."

Grace turned to her. "Why? Because she's deaf?"

Miss Louise nodded. "We worry about Joanna's deafness in public. Some people are very insensitive. Surely your aunt knows that."

A memory flashed into Grace's mind: Mama and Aunt

Emma in the market, signing to each other about tomatoes, when a boy pointed and called out, "Dummies!" Mama hollered back at the boy, and when she raised her fist, he ran away. But Aunt Emma was quiet, her face crumpled with pain. Grace knew the boy had hurt her feelings.

"Is that why Mr. Hammond doesn't want Joanna to sign?" Grace asked.

Miss Louise seemed surprised at the question.

"Esterbelle told me," Grace said.

Miss Louise frowned, but she nodded, too. "Yes. Father thinks that signing draws attention, and he and Mother don't want anyone teasing or making fun of Joanna."

"Does that mean I shouldn't sign to Joanna anymore?" Grace asked.

"No. We all sign to Joanna. It's just that Father wants her to be able to read lips, too. But the deafness, Grace—it's not the only reason Joanna doesn't go out. We also worry about her picking up germs. She was very sick as a child. When she was four, she had scarlet fever and almost died. In fact, that's how she lost her hearing. Now the minute she gets a cold we worry about pneumonia."

"Mama says the fresh air is good for you," Grace said.

"Joanna *does* get outside," Miss Louise assured her. "She goes to church with us. And every Saturday afternoon she visits a woman who is working with her on lipreading and teaching her how to sew."

"Twice a week?" Grace wasn't sure she heard right.

Miss Louise seemed to know what she was thinking. "She has a good life, Grace. She'll never be hungry. She has a nice room of her own—with shelves full of puzzles and books and paints. A closet full of lovely clothes. Not to mention a family that loves her *very* much."

Grace was speechless. She could not find fault with any of that. It would be wonderful indeed not to ever feel hunger in the night. To wake up smelling cinnamon and have all those lovely things Joanna had stacked on her shelves and in her closet. She glanced back at the empty doorway. Even if you *were* lonely.

MEASURING MAGIC

At the corner near the zoo, Grace and Miss Louise caught the trolley and took it downtown, where they walked through the busy streets to Woodward and Lothrop's Department Store. Inside, the huge store buzzed with activity and brimmed with holiday decorations. Every counter they passed had something exquisite: silk scarves, wallets, leather gloves, veiled hats, fuzzy imitation-lamb mufflers.

In the children's department, Miss Louise gathered an armful of dresses and accompanied Grace to the dressing room.

"You look like a princess!" Miss Louise exclaimed, tying a white sash at the waist of a red velvet dress. "Grace, it'll be perfect for Christmas day."

Grace twirled around and couldn't stop looking at herself in the mirror.

Two other dresses were selected for everyday wear, then shoes that fit properly, boots for rain and snow, a navy blue coat with large black buttons, and a fuzzy white pom-pom hat with a matching scarf and mittens. Miss Louise also purchased a whole pile of new white underwear for Grace, and several pairs of soft woolen stockings.

Laden with their bags and boxes, the two rode the elevator to the seventh-floor tearoom, where Miss Louise said they would "get a bite to eat." Grace couldn't begin to imagine how much money had already been spent. And now lunch?

The tearoom was all aglitter with silver tinsel and big red bows. Each table was covered with a green tablecloth, a glass bowl full of holly, and white napkins rolled into gold star napkin rings.

After being seated by a waiter, Grace opened her menu, but the handwriting was so fancy, she had to struggle to read it: baked fresh ham and lettuced—no, *latticed*—potatoes, eggs stuffed with fresh shrimp in salad, or chicken shortcake topped with currant jelly. Each was followed by the notation *75 cents*.

Seventy-five cents was a lot of money, Grace thought. Did Miss Louise mean for her to choose an entire lunch for herself? Her mouth began to water just thinking about chicken shortcake. But seventy-five cents? Could that be right? Grace and her mother would spend an entire day washing Mrs. Hewitt's clothes to earn that much.

At the bottom of the card, Grace read that dessert was included with the luncheon: lemon chiffon pie or fudge cake with hazelnut cream filling.

"Are you ready to order?" Miss Louise asked Grace.

How could Grace eat all this wonderful food when Mama and Papa were probably grilling stale bread in old grease? Her eyes fell away from the menu and her stomach grew tight.

"Grace, are you ready?"

A lump grew in the back of Grace's throat. But what good would it do *not* to eat? Besides, she was hungry. She had to eat something.

"Grace, are you okay?"

She looked up at Miss Louise. "Chicken shortcake," she said in a small voice. "Please," she added, remembering her manners.

Miss Louise turned to the waiter. "We'll have two chicken shortcakes, a glass of milk, and one cup of coffee."

Grace slipped the gold star off her cloth napkin and fumbled at her side for the pocket in her dress. Then carefully, she smoothed out the wide square of white linen on her lap.

While they ate, Miss Louise asked Grace a lot of questions. Was she a good student in school? What were her favorite foods? Did she get sick a lot?

"I always get good grades on account of Pete's help," Grace replied. "I love everything 'cept lima beans. . . . And I ain't hardly ever been sick—only once with chicken pox. I remember because my papa rubbed a salve all over me that stunk to high heaven and made me cry like a stuck pig."

Miss Louise winced a little, and Grace didn't know if it was because of what she said or because some bad grammar was slipping in there again. Darn. Grace knew not to use the word *ain't*. Mama always said, "That's how the ignorant talk." And she did *not* want to sound ignorant.

"You know, when I first saw you, Grace, I thought you

were younger. Nine maybe. My daughter would have been nine. . . ." Miss Louise suddenly stopped and seemed to catch herself. "So what do you like to do for fun, Grace?"

Grace didn't hesitate. "Fish," she replied.

"Fish? You mean with a pole?"

"*And* a hook!" Grace giggled at Miss Louise's expression. "You haven't ever been fishing, Miss Louise?"

Miss Louise smiled and shook her head. "Never."

"Well, me and Pete and Papa will take you sometime, then. We know a real good spot on the Potomac where you can catch carp this big." Grace opened her arms (exaggerating quite a lot). "It's tons of fun, Miss Louise."

"That would be nice," Miss Louise said politely, placing her fork and knife on the luncheon plate to indicate she had finished.

Grace eyed the generous portion of chicken and biscuit that Miss Louise had left uneaten.

"Listen, I hear Santa Claus is in the toy department today." Miss Louise raised her eyebrows. "Would you like to visit?"

Grace didn't think it would be polite to ask Miss Louise for the rest of her uneaten chicken. But it sure looked good. She forced her eyes off the plate and swallowed hard.

"Would you?" Miss Louise repeated.

Santa Claus. Miss Louise had asked her about seeing Santa Claus. Grace tried to think how she would reply because she did not believe in Santa Claus. How could she when last year there had been *nothing* for any of them on Christmas morning?

"I don't mind waiting," Miss Louise insisted.

Grace contemplated her answer as the waiter took away

their luncheon dishes and set down two plates with thick slices of fudge cake. The piece was big enough for four people, she thought. Grace began to seriously consider the possibility that if Miss Louise really was some sort of guardian angel, then maybe Santa Claus was real, too. Or maybe he was real for some children but not for others. Was there a way to measure magic? Had Grace already had her share of it?

Grace, still awed by the cake, picked up her fork and looked back to Miss Louise. "If you like," she said shyly.

Miss Louise sat back, beaming.

The cake was delicious and Grace ate every bite. She could still taste the rich, dark chocolate as she stood in line to see Santa Claus. She waited for a long time with lots of children, including a whiny little boy in front of her who bore a striking resemblance to Owen. He kept asking his mother how much longer; then he'd sniff, wipe his nose on his cuff, and turn to stare up at Grace. Grace ignored him, however, and resented him all the more for the fine clothes he wore: the corduroy suit jacket and the new plaid knickers. Owen had never known clothes as nice as that. She stared over his head full of curls and rehearsed in her mind exactly what she would request: *A home for my family. A job for my papa. A cure for Pete.*

Finally, when it was her turn, Grace boldly took a seat on Santa's lap.

"And what can I bring this young lady?" Santa Claus asked.

Miss Louise leaned forward to hear.

Grace hesitated, while Santa Claus dropped his chin and looked over his glasses at her, because she also wanted a doll to replace the one she had lost.

Thoughts were swirling through Grace's mind: What if Santa Claus *was* real? What if he really did get children the things they wanted?

Santa Claus bounced her on his knee. "What'll it be, young lady?"

"A doll," Grace blurted out. "A doll with lots of clothes."

"Oh, ho! Ho! Ho!" Santa Claus laughed. A big fake laugh, Grace thought. "I'll see what the elves can do!"

Grace panicked. "Three other things," she hastened to add.

"Oh! I think that's quite enough for one little girl, don't you?" Santa Claus pressed a gold coin with his picture on it into her hand.

And Grace hurried to get away.

On the trolley going home, it bothered Grace that she had asked for a doll first when she should have asked Santa Claus to help her family. Or cure Pete. Or find a job for Papa.

Pete would say she was too old for a doll. But Grace wanted a doll. *I deserve a doll,* she told herself. *Even those girls at the mission had dolls! Why not me?*

The trolley moved quickly. Cold air came and went when the door opened. Grace chewed on her bottom lip.

"You have such a serious look on your face," Miss Louise said. She folded her hands over the pocketbook on her lap. "It's supposed to warm up a little tomorrow. Would you like to go to the zoo?"

Grace turned her head slightly to stare out the window. Santa Claus *wasn't* real, she told herself. It didn't matter. It was okay to ask for a doll.

"We could take Esterbelle—and go see the baby elephant," Miss Louise said. "Would you like that?"

Grace nodded, realizing something had been said about the zoo. But inside, she still felt bad for what she had done.

At home in the Hammond house, Grace hung up her three new dresses and her coat in the closet and laid out the rest of the things on her bed.

"You can change out of that green dress if you like." Miss Louise plucked out a hat pin, removed her stylish velvet hat, and checked her hair in the mirror. "Go ahead, put on a new one. Do you have a favorite?"

Grace shook her head. "No, I love everything."

"Good!" Miss Louise unclipped her pearl earrings and leaned in toward the mirror to freshen her lipstick, then pressed her lips together. "Well, I'm going to help Mother get dinner ready. Take your time, Grace."

"I will."

When she was alone, Grace picked up her new white hat and sat on the edge of the bed. The white pom-pom was silky and reminded Grace of the rabbit. Her eyes blurred. She glanced back at her new dresses and wondered what Mama would say about all these new clothes? Would she be happy? Or would she and Papa be angry because Grace had accepted so many things from a stranger?

Papa always said he didn't like taking charity. He hated to stand in line for free bags of flour. But weren't they all happy when the box of food from church arrived on Thanksgiving? The canned ham was good and salty, and Mama rationed out that hunk of orange cheese for weeks.

Suddenly, Grace was aware that Joanna stood in the doorway.

"Come in," Grace said, standing and beckoning with her hand.

As Joanna approached, she pointed at Grace and made a sign with her hands coming down in front of her face.

Grace didn't understand.

"Sad?" Joanna finger spelled.

Grace nodded. "Miss my family," she finger spelled back.

Joanna's eyes filled with compassion.

"Especially my brother, Pete. I worry," she said, looking at Joanna and hoping she understood.

Joanna began to finger spell, and, slowly, Grace translated out loud. "I . . .know . . . where . . . is . . . hospital. . . . See . . ." She pointed at Grace. "Brother," she finished.

Grace looked from Joanna's hand to her face. "You know where the Tuberculosis Hospital is?"

Joanna nodded.

Why was Joanna telling her this?

"Miss Louise says I can't visit there," Grace said, shaking her head. "Are you saying we *can?*"

Joanna made the sign for *yes*, which was to move her closed right fist up and down like a little head, nodding as well.

"How?" Grace asked.

But just then, the heavy front door closed. Grace heard Esterbelle's voice, then heard her feet running up the stairs.

Joanna put a finger to her lips.

"Be quiet?" Grace was confused.

Joanna tapped her lips as Esterbelle burst into the room.

"You're back!" Grace tried to sound cheerful.

Esterbelle stopped, her eyes scanning all the things spread out on the bed. "Is all this *yours?*"

"Can you believe it? Miss Louise bought all these things for me at a big store downtown. We had lunch in the tearoom, too," Grace said, although she skipped the part about Santa Claus.

"Joanna." Grace caught her arm. "You don't have to go."

But Joanna pulled away and left.

"She doesn't like me," Esterbelle said. "I don't know why. I guess because we can't communicate."

"You could learn to finger spell. It's not very hard."

Esterbelle wrinkled her nose. "I don't think so. It's too complicated." Picking up Grace's new scarf, Esterbelle let the tassels run through her fingers. "So why did Miss Louise buy you all these clothes?"

Grace watched her. "She told me it was a gift."

Esterbelle touched the edge of the new coat then, and Grace recognized the envious look on her face. There had been plenty of times when Grace had felt the same, longing for some of the nice things other girls at school had.

"I can't even remember when I got something brand-new," Grace hastened to add. "All my clothes are hand-me-downs. Even my shoes!"

"This hat is yours, too?" Esterbelle asked. She picked up the new hat and squeezed the silky pom-pom.

"You should have seen my old one!" Grace exclaimed. "Used to belong to my brother Pete till his head got too big. It's got a moth hole bigger'n a silver dollar in it!"

Esterbelle set the hat down and narrowed her eyes. "They're not going to adopt you, are they? I mean, where would you sleep? You can't stay in Miss Betsy's room."

"Adopt me? What are you talking about?" Grace stared at her. "I have a family, Esterbelle. I'm here for Christmas is all."

"Esterbelle!" Mrs. Scarlotti called. "Where are you? I need help with these packages!"

Esterbelle rolled her eyes. "Guess I have to go," she said.

Grace was glad. She closed the door behind Esterbelle. But as she changed out of the green dress and began to pull on the new red corduroy one, she began to wonder. Was it possible Miss Louise *did* want to adopt her? Did Mama and Papa know about this? Were these clothes just a gift?

The new red dress slipped over her head and fell softly, settling perfectly on her shoulders and at her waist.

Maybe Miss Louise wanted Grace to replace the little girl who had died, Grace thought. But why wouldn't she want another baby instead?

While she reached behind to tie her bow, Grace wondered what it would be like to live here, in the Hammonds' house, with a closet full of beautiful dresses and shelves stacked with books, games, and puzzles.

If you were adopted, did you get to see your real family, too?

Frowning, she pulled on the end of one braid. How could anyone leave his or her real family to go live with another one? Even if your real family was poor and didn't have a place to live, or much to eat, it didn't seem right. . . .

Catching her reflection in the full-length mirror beside Miss

Betsy's bed, Grace slowly straightened up and flipped her braids back over her shoulders. She turned sideways to see how the bow looked in back, then swung her hips to see how the skirt fell in front. Back and forth she turned, admiring herself in the fine, new corduroy dress.

SECRETS

Y̶ou should have *seen* some of those other children, crying and carrying on! You'd have thought the man was Al Capone—or a dentist in disguise!" Miss Louise had everyone at dinner that night chuckling over her description of the children waiting in line to see Santa Claus.

"Grace, though, she marched right up there. Didn't you?" Miss Louise leaned back so everyone could see Grace.

Shyly, from her seat beside Miss Louise, Grace nodded and looked back to her plate, where she was twirling spaghetti onto her fork. She was a little uncomfortable being the center of attention because no one had ever talked about her this way—not even Mama. Not that Mama didn't appreciate her! It's just that there was so much to be done at home—there wasn't time to go around heaping this kind of attention on any one of them.

But it sure did feel nice listening to Miss Louise go on and on about her, Grace thought, unable to resist smiling. It was as though every little thing she had done was utterly wonderful.

"Well, it sounds as though you girls had a swell time,"

Johnny said, winking at Grace. He reached across the table to squeeze Miss Louise's hand. "You look so pretty when you smile," he whispered to her.

Grace pushed a fork full of noodles into her mouth so Mr. Johnny didn't think she was eavesdropping.

Joanna tapped Miss Louise on the arm and pointed to Grace, and Miss Louise repeated, to Grace's embarrassment, the bit about Santa Claus. The clear, distinct way she spoke for Joanna's benefit underscored Grace's guilt: "Grace told Santa Claus she wanted a doll with lots of clothes."

Joanna peered around her sister so she could see Grace, and smiled.

When dinner was over, the girls helped to dry dishes in the kitchen.

Grace would have preferred returning to the living room, where Mr. Hammond was tuning in the radio and Johnny and Joanna were setting up a card table. But on their way out of the kitchen, Esterbelle whispered urgently, "I need to talk to you."

"You need to talk to *me?*" Grace asked.

"Now," Esterbelle emphasized.

Reluctant, but curious, Grace followed Esterbelle upstairs to Mr. Hammond's study, a small room filled with books and a large oak rolltop desk. Esterbelle sat heavily in Mr. Hammond's big leather-seated swivel chair and made it spin in a circle.

"Won't Mr. Hammond be angry?" Grace asked, standing in the doorway.

Esterbelle grabbed the edge of the desk and brought the chair to a stop. "How's he going to know? He'd never leave *The Fred Allen Show.*"

When Grace didn't move, Esterbelle rolled her eyes. "All right," she agreed, sliding off the chair. She sat on the carpet and patted the spot in front of her until Grace sat down.

"Now. If you want to be friends while you're here, we have to trust each other," Esterbelle said matter-of-factly. "Here's how we're going to prove our trust. *You*, Grace, have to think of something secret to tell me, something you have never told anyone. And I will tell *you* something no one else knows."

"But I don't have any secrets," Grace said, opening her hands.

Esterbelle didn't blink an eye. "Everyone has secrets, Grace. Everyone has something they don't want anyone else to know! Especially in *this* house!"

"What do you mean?"

She shook back her long, dark curls. "I'll give you an example," Esterbelle said. "Take Swede. He tells everyone he's a salesman, but *phooey!* Do you know what he *really* does? He sells flowers on the street corner. It's true, because Mother and I saw him." She cupped her hands around her mouth and called out softly: "Roses! Three cents each!" She smirked. "*Hmmpf!* And he tells everyone he's a salesman."

Grace instantly felt sorry for the cheerful, chubby man in the three-piece suit. "He's just trying to make a living."

"But he's a fake!" Esterbelle retorted, her dark eyes flashing. "He isn't what he says he is. So, I'm sure you can think of something." Esterbelle was not going to give up. "Miss Louise is taking us to the zoo tomorrow. We'll exchange there, okay?"

Mrs. Scarlotti was calling. "Ester! Where are you, dear?"

Esterbelle groaned and pushed herself up. "Remember. *Tomorrow*," she said before disappearing out the door.

Grace stood up after she had gone and was glad she hadn't committed herself to Esterbelle's dumb idea of exchanging secrets. But she wondered if Esterbelle was right, about everyone having a secret.

Once, when Grace was crouched behind the big gas stove in the kitchen, where she warmed her feet, she overheard her mother confide in a neighbor how she wished she would lose the new baby before it was born. She said they couldn't afford to feed another child. The neighbor—Mrs. Ferguson—must have reached over and grabbed Mama's wrist because there was a slapping noise against the table. *Ruth, don't ever say that again!* Mama was already weeping, but Mrs. Ferguson kept on. *And don't you dare tell Clement. He does his best to keep you all going.*

Hugging her knees, Grace had waited, not wanting her mother or Mrs. Ferguson to know she had overheard.

Grace picked at a hangnail on her thumb. There were more secrets. Mama being German. The way she and Pete took things—*stole things*, really. Papa making corn liquor—although she could never tell anyone about that! Not for any reason. Because she had promised Pete, because she didn't want Papa to be in jail—and because Grace knew that the man with the sharp blade who caught them watching might still come after them if he found out.

There were a lot of secrets tucked away inside Grace.

But none that she wanted to share with Esterbelle.

In the elephant barn at the zoo the next day, the smell was so pungent, Grace and Esterbelle had to hold their noses. Even

Miss Louise covered part of her face with a gloved hand. "I know it's cold out, girls, but I do wish someone would open a door once in a while."

Grace and Esterbelle giggled. They agreed, but neither one of them wanted to leave. They had fallen in love with the baby elephant.

"Look how many wrinkles he has!" Esterbelle said, pointing. "He's just like a miniature *old* elephant."

"He's so shy, too," Grace noted. "See? He doesn't want to leave his mother. They're holding trunks!"

"Bye-bye, baby elephant!"

"Merry Christmas!" the girls' voices chimed sweetly.

"Oh, Miss Louise," Grace said, "you should have let Joanna come. She would *love* that baby elephant!"

"You're right." She put her arm around Grace and squeezed her shoulders. "She would love him to pieces, wouldn't she? When she's over that cold of hers, we'll bring her to see him."

Grace surprised herself by putting her arms around Miss Louise and hugging her back. Miss Louise seemed so small compared to Mama. Grace could reach almost all the way around her. She smelled good, too. Not too flowery, like Miss Betsy.

Outside the elephant barn, Grace squinted from the bright sun; and on their way through the melting snow to visit the tigers, Miss Louise bought a bag of popcorn for them to share. It was the day before Christmas, and the girls already had been warned it would be a short visit.

"Can you wait while I use the ladies' room?" Miss Louise asked.

Grace and Esterbelle nodded and sat on a nearby bench.

"It'll be fun making cookies today," Grace said, swinging her feet beneath the wooden seat. "Miss Louise said we could decorate them."

"I know. And I can't wait until Christmas morning. I already counted six presents for me under that tree—and Santa Claus hasn't even come yet! There are at least two gifts for you, Grace. Plus we'll hang stockings."

"Do you think so?" Grace stopped swinging her legs and smiled as she stomped her feet in her new boots to warm up her toes.

"Have you decided?" Esterbelle asked.

Grace knew she meant the secret. She scrunched her nose and shook her head. "Not yet," she said, sitting on her hands.

Then, right there at the zoo, without any kind of warning, Esterbelle made a startling revelation: "My secret is that my father ran away with another woman. A gypsy!"

Astonished, Grace turned to Esterbelle. She couldn't imagine her own father running away with another woman. Papa might be impatient and have a fierce temper sometimes, but he loved Mama. He even brought Mama a basket of strawberries on her last birthday, and Mama cried because she said he couldn't afford to do that.

"It's true," Esterbelle went on. "My father doesn't write us or anything. He lost all our money in the stock-market crash, and then he took off."

"That's terrible," Grace said, pulling her hands out from under her.

Esterbelle pressed her fingers together. "I told you.

Everybody has secrets. I bet I know a secret about everyone in that boardinghouse."

"You do?" Grace couldn't help herself.

"I know Mr. Parker isn't really writing a novel. He types the same sentence over and over again every day, just so it sounds like he's working."

Grace frowned. How would Esterbelle know that unless she snuck into Mr. Parker's room?

"Mother says *that's* because he has writer's block, but he's too proud to admit it. Besides, there's no one to buy his stories anymore. His publisher went out of business. Mother said so."

Grace winced. It embarrassed her to hear these things.

Esterbelle peered at Grace sideways. "I also know that Miss Louise and Mr. Johnny can't have children."

Grace looked at her. "Why not?"

Esterbelle shrugged. "They don't know. They had a baby once, but it died. Now Miss Louise can't have any more children. That's why they want to adopt someone. They tried once before—a little girl named Nellie. Only she cried all the time and kept getting sick, so they took her back to the mission."

"So you think she wants to adopt *me?*" Grace screwed up her face. "I'm not an orphan!"

"That woman at the mission, she said all the children there come from poor families. She told Miss Louise that anyone who got adopted out of that mission should consider themselves lucky. I heard Miss Louise herself tell that to Mr. Johnny."

"But what if I don't *want* to stay?" Grace asked.

"Suit yourself. You don't have to. Miss Louise and Mr. Johnny would never keep someone here who didn't want to stay. They're too nice. I mean, look—they took back Nellie, didn't they?"

Grace was shocked by the information.

"It took a lot of courage for Miss Louise to go and get you," Esterbelle continued with an air of superiority. "You see, she's afraid she can't ever love a child again. On account of losing her own little girl."

Grace felt an enormous pang of sympathy for Miss Louise, who probably had *no idea* that Esterbelle had been eavesdropping and exposing these deeply personal matters.

Esterbelle smiled complacently. "I told you. I know something about *everybody*—shy little Joanna, too. She's quite the little writer, Miss Joanna. Mrs. Hammond would *die* if she knew what she was doing."

"What are you talking about?"

A smug expression consumed Esterbelle's delicate features. "Every Saturday when the tutor sends her son, Mr. Jimmy, to take Joanna home, they go places instead: the library, the art museum, the coffee shop. Joanna calls them her 'little adventures.'"

Grace's fascination with the information suddenly turned to anger. "You're making this up!" she accused. "You're making all this up!"

"I'm *not.*"

"You're a *liar*, Esterbelle!"

"I'm *not* a liar!" Esterbelle shot back. "Joanna wrote it in her diary."

"And *you* read her diary?"

Esterbelle shook back her hair. "One day I found it," she said. "It was on the window seat upstairs. I didn't know it was hers until I read some of it."

Grace drew back, disgusted, and turned to see if Miss Louise was coming out of the rest room yet.

An uncomfortable moment stretched between them.

Esterbelle sighed. "Joanna's so sad," she said, flicking some snow off her coat sleeve. "I feel sorry for her. Don't you?"

Grace confronted Esterbelle with a scowl. "Why? Because she's deaf?"

"Well, how would *you* like it if you could never hear music? Or what people were saying to you?"

Grace twisted her mouth. "My aunt Emma's deaf, and nobody feels sorry for her! And you know what? I don't think it's such a big deal that Joanna goes places with her tutor. She's fourteen years old!"

Esterbelle's eyes flashed. "But if Mrs. Hammond knew, she wouldn't ever let Joanna out of the house again!"

"Well, you're not going to tell her, are you?"

"I will if you don't share, Grace. You have to tell me *your* secret now or it's not fair."

Grace turned away and stared at the ground in front of her again, to where her stomping had made an indentation in the wet snow. Very slowly, she pushed on it with the toe of her boot to make it deeper. She didn't want to share any of her secrets with Esterbelle. She didn't trust Esterbelle.

But neither did Grace want Esterbelle squealing about Joanna's adventures. Besides all that, how could she *not* share something after hearing about Esterbelle's father? A gypsy. How *awful* for her.

Esterbelle leaned back on the bench.

It probably wouldn't hurt, Grace figured. "Well, I . . ."

When she paused, Esterbelle sat up and prodded. "What?"

Grace cleared her throat. "I stole some things."

Esterbelle bit her bottom lip and scooted closer.

"Back at the apartments where I used to live," Grace said. "I stole a watch. My brother and I did. We pawned it."

"What else?" Esterbelle pressed. "Miss Betsy has a lot of nice stuff in her room. Did you sneak something of hers? I promise not to tell—cross my heart and hope to die, stick a needle in my eye!"

Grace felt her eyes widen and her blood turn to ice. Did Esterbelle know about the pin? Heck, if she snuck into Mr. Parker's room, then she had probably already rooted through Grace's stuff, too! She'd probably *seen* the list—*and* the brooch!

"I was going to—but I'm putting it back!" Grace hastened to explain.

"I knew it! It was jewelry, wasn't it?" Esterbelle demanded.

"That star pin," Grace confessed in a small voice.

Esterbelle's mouth dropped. "The one with diamonds?"

"I'm putting it back," Grace insisted, swearing to herself she would return it the instant she went to her room. "*Honest* I am."

Satisfied at last, Esterbelle shut her mouth and leaned back against the bench, crossing her arms.

Grace already regretted everything she'd said, and a sick feeling settled in her stomach.

"It's not much of a secret compared to yours," Grace said,

trying to shift the attention back to Esterbelle. "I'm sorry your father ran away with a gypsy."

Esterbelle stared off into the distance. Then, suddenly, she was reaching toward Grace. Did she want to hold hands? Maybe, since they had shared secrets, the tiny seeds of a true friendship had been sown. Maybe this was how it happened. Still wary, Grace pulled her hands apart and opened her fingers.

But Esterbelle was simply after another handful of popcorn.

CHRISTMAS

Grace awoke with a start and remembered right away that it was Christmas. Downstairs, at least two gifts waited for her under the glittering branches of the tree.

Curling her fingers and toes in anticipation, she turned her head against the pillow to look over at the bed across the room. Miss Betsy was still asleep, however. All that could be seen was the scalloped collar of her nightgown and the back of her head with rows of perfect brown waves tucked neatly beneath the hair net she wore at night.

Frustrated that it was so early, Grace rolled onto her back and pulled the afghan up to her chin. But it was no use trying to sleep. Her eyes wandered across the plaster ceiling and the fancy molding, on down to the windows, where she studied the intricate design in the lace curtains. The lace reminded Grace of tree branches and how, last summer, when it was too hot to sleep, she and Pete took quilts and made a bed on the roof of the apartment building. It was cool on the roof, camped out next to the pigeons, staring up through the dark branches that sprawled against the moonlit sky like black Spanish lace.

Grace remembered searching for a falling star to wish upon, and Pete rattling on about baseball. . . .

"He's just not a great manager. I'm not puttin' him down, Grace. No way. Walter Johnson was a great pitcher. Do you know he delivered that ball so fast, they used to call him the 'Big Train'?"

"They did?"

"Grace, Walter Johnson won 416 games, and 110 of them were shutouts. Think about that! Now that's a record to be proud of. First game Papa ever took me to at Griffith Stadium, Walter Johnson pitched a shutout. I'll never forget it, no sir, not till the day I die."

A smile curled Grace's lips, remembering Pete and his baseball. He loved the game, even though his arm kept him from playing sandlot ball with the neighborhood boys. He liked to pitch, though. He would pitch balls to Papa for hours on a Saturday afternoon. If Papa had to work, then Pete would pitch to Grace. One time, in the backyard on Maryland Avenue, Grace smacked the ball right through the open upstairs window and into the rocking chair, where Mama was nursing Owen.

Mama wasn't angry. Mama hardly ever got angry. Not even on those nights when Papa didn't come home until dawn. Instead, she kept the little boys quiet so Papa could sleep. It made Grace wonder: Did Mama know he was making corn liquor with those other men? Maybe it wasn't a secret from Mama. If she did know, didn't she worry he'd get caught and thrown in jail?

Grace's mind spun: If Mama knew about Papa, then did she know about the rabbit, too? After all, she was the one who cooked it. Papa told them it was chicken from the market. It was months before Grace knew the truth.

Her lip began to tremble. They never would have had to eat the rabbit if they hadn't all been so hungry. Owen and Iggy, holding their tummies and crying into Mama's skirt . . . Tears pooled in her eyes. Deep in her heart Grace knew why Papa did it. He did it because he was trying to take care of them. And really, when you got right down to it, it wasn't anything worse than what she and Pete had done, stealing those things.

Grace was sorry all over again that she had asked Santa Claus for a doll. Her face grew warm with shame, and tears swelled in the corners of her eyes.

Suddenly, the bedroom door opened with a squeak. Esterbelle, her hair mussed from sleep, stuck her head in. "Do you want to go downstairs?" she asked in a loud whisper.

Grace wiped her eyes with the edge of her pillowcase and pushed herself up.

"Merry Christmas, girls," Miss Betsy said sleepily.

"Please, Miss Betsy," Esterbelle said in her sweetest voice, "may Grace and I go downstairs and empty our stockings?"

"Yes, I think that would be okay."

Grace sat on the edge of the bed uncertainly. How could she go empty a stocking full of wonderful things when her two little brothers were in a mission with cold floors and cranky Miss Mabel—and Pete was lying who knows where?

"It's okay, Grace," Miss Betsy repeated. "Go on down with Esterbelle."

"Come *on!*" Esterbelle urged.

Christmas. Grace rose and followed Esterbelle out the door. Then, holding her nightgown above her ankles to keep from tripping, Grace allowed herself to be swept up in the excitement and rushed down the stairs.

The stockings they had hung the night before bulged with treasures. Together, the girls settled cross-legged on the rug to discover what Santa Claus had left.

"Oh, goodie! A comic book!" Esterbelle squealed. "Did you get one, too, Grace?"

"Yes, *The Shadow*," she said, unrolling her copy.

"And some jacks—and a comb and brush! My set is blue. Did you get a comb and brush? What color, Grace?"

"Pink—a pink set. I have jacks, too. And look—beautiful hair clips."

Tucked away in the stockings were also Necco wafers, chocolate bars, peppermint sticks, and small rulers. The girls piled up their goodies as others slowly drifted into the room, talking quietly.

Miss Louise sat with a cup of coffee in the chair nearest Grace. And soon Joanna, too old for a stocking, was there, too, perched on the sofa, watching with Miss Betsy's arm around her.

When the stockings were emptied and breakfast was eaten, everyone reassembled in the living room to open presents. Grace marveled at the gifts: silk stockings for Mrs. Scarlotti, a bottle of Evening in Paris perfume for Miss Betsy (from which she gave Grace, Esterbelle, and Joanna each a cool, fragrant dab behind their ears). Mr. Hammond opened up a soft alpaca auto robe and spread it out over his lap. "I'd like to borrow your roadster, Johnny," he said, "and take a nice long ride on that new Skyline Drive everyone is talking about."

Esterbelle unwrapped roller skates, a new sweater, and paper dolls, among other things, then scooped up everything and rushed off with her mother to get dressed and catch a train to Danville, Virginia, where they would stay with relatives for a few days.

For Joanna, there was a new book, a silver locket, a tablet of drawing paper, and several pretty hair ribbons.

And for Grace, new mittens and watercolor paints. "I'll teach you," Joanna finger spelled. And—the best gift of all—a beautiful doll with curly brown hair. With the doll came three dresses with miniature buttons, a small coat, and a soft flannel nightgown. Grace loved the doll. She lifted it from the tissue and held it close.

Soon, a huge pile of wrapping paper and ribbon had accumulated in the middle of the living-room floor. So many wonderful things had been opened, it was hard to keep up with everything. Johnny sat with a new Philco radio on his lap, but then set it down to show Mr. Parker how to use his Zippo lighter. Mr. Hammond was busy reading aloud the instructions to Mrs. Hammond's Hoover vacuum cleaner, and Swede was holding up the box to his new jigsaw puzzle—a picture of New York Harbor and the Statue of Liberty. He said he would start it that day, if Grace and Joanna would help.

"That looks like the end of it," Mr. Hammond announced, leaning forward to peer under the tree.

But it was not the end of it. Far from it, Grace thought. The entire day was a continuous stream of gifts. The roasted turkey;

the three kinds of pie; the attention lavished on her by Miss Louise; the fun she had with Joanna, piecing together the puzzle in front of the fire.

If only, she thought, Iggy and Owen could be here, too, gobbling up Christmas cookies one after the other and ripping open wonderful presents. If Pete were here, he'd never be cold. He'd get better in a week if he could sit by the fire and drink lots of hot chocolate. And Mama and Papa? Grace's eyes grew misty. . . .

"I think I see one," Miss Louise said, reaching over Grace's shoulder for a tiny puzzle piece, which she snapped into place.

Grace smiled wanly—and watched Miss Louise select another piece and place it in the right spot.

"How'd you do that?" Grace asked, incredulous.

"It was that little tip of red there, see?"

Joanna patted the table and motioned for Miss Louise to sit down.

"Yes, will you stay and help us?" Grace asked.

Miss Louise seemed pleased to be asked. "Certainly," she said, setting down her cup of tea and pulling a chair over to the card table.

"We're looking for edges so we can finish the border," Grace told her.

But just as Miss Louise sat down, Mr. Hammond came to the doorway and called to Grace. "Young lady," he said, extending a yellow envelope. "You have a telegram."

Grace remained sitting. Who would send *her* a telegram? Telegrams brought bad news, didn't they? She glanced around quickly at everyone. Grace didn't want bad news. She didn't want *any* news.

Mr. Hammond could see that she was uncertain.

"Would you like me to read it first?" he asked kindly.

"Yes, please," Grace said timidly.

Miss Louise reached over the card table and placed her hand on Grace's. They waited silently as Mr. Hammond tore open the envelope and scanned the message. "Looks like Grace has one more gift," he said, handing the telegram to her with a reassuring smile.

MERRY CHRISTMAS STOP YOU HAVE A SISTER NAMED
HOLLY NOEL STOP MAMA PAPA BABY FINE STOP LOVE
UNCLE STEWART

No Windows

It was Miss Louise's idea. Several days after Christmas she asked Grace, "Would you like to visit your parents? Mrs. Claiborne at the mission tells me they've found a new apartment. We can take them some food—and you can see your baby sister."

Grace was surprised at the offer but hesitated before nodding yes.

Miss Louise cocked her head. "Are you sure?"

"Yes. Yes, I'm sure," Grace said.

But the truth was that inside, Grace had mixed feelings. The past few days had been packed with fun: trips to the National Theater to see a play and the Martha Washington candy store for licorice; card games in front of the fire; and songs at the piano with Miss Betsy and Joanna, who enjoyed the music by holding her palms flat on the piano top so she could feel its vibrations.

Grace knew when Mama and Papa were resettled, it would be time to go home again. And in a thoroughly secret thought—deep, *deep* inside—this disappointed her. After all, she'd gotten used to three wonderful meals a day and a soft warm, rollaway bed. And she loved Joanna's quiet companionship and the way Miss Louise doted on them both. Who wouldn't want that to continue for just a while longer?

But it was not the only reason Grace was hesitant. And the day they actually packed up some food to take with them to see Mama and Papa, Grace began to worry all over again.

"Why so glum?" Mrs. Hammond tugged on one of Grace's braids before handing her a jar of apple jelly for the food box. "Aren't you excited about going to see your little sister?"

Grace tried to smile. "I *am* happy," she said as she took the jelly. It wasn't a lie; part of her *was* happy. After all, she was going to see Mama and Papa again—and she had always wanted a sister.

Mrs. Hammond handed Grace another jar, this one blackberry jam, and Grace nestled it in between cans of cranberry sauce and green beans. Babies were cute, she was thinking. She remembered Iggy's miniature fingers and toes with their tiny wrinkles, his little pug nose, and the delicate fuzz on his head.

Joanna balled up another piece of newspaper and playfully tossed it to Grace so she could push it into the spaces between the jars. Grace wondered if Holly Noel would smile the first time she saw her big sister—or did smiles come later? Grace couldn't remember.

"Now these we want on top," Mrs. Hammond said, settling a basket of rolls wrapped in a clean dish towel atop the cans and jars.

Miss Louise had bought a little pink sweater for the new baby. The sweater was almost small enough to fit Grace's new doll. That's how small babies were when they were born. "Johnny will carry the turkey," Mrs. Hammond instructed Miss Louise. "And the pie ought to be carried separately, too."

Over it all, the bigger question had loomed: What would another baby mean to Mama? A baby was one more mouth to feed. More diapers to change. More laundry to wash and dry.

Grace placed a tin of chocolate fudge on top of the crumpled newspaper and stood staring into the box.

Outside, Johnny's car was warmed up and waiting, its exhaust making a tall plume of swirling gray air. Grace wore her new red velvet Christmas dress and sat in the backseat beside the turkey, the pie in her lap and her doll beside her.

As they crossed a bridge over Rock Creek, Grace looked down at the frozen water and snow-covered branches far below. When they passed the foreign embassies along Connecticut Avenue, she marveled at the fancy iron gates and paved driveways lined with shiny black cars.

In a short time the scenery changed, however, to streets lined with unkempt buildings with boarded-up windows and sidewalks piled with trash.

"This is it," Johnny said as he slowed the car and pulled over. Miss Louise rechecked the address and peered doubtfully at the four-story building.

Two wild cats ran away as they approached. Inside the front door, they entered a dimly lit, paint-chipped hallway.

"Your uncle Stewart said the apartment was a subbasement unit. That means your parents are beneath the basement," Miss Louise said, eyeing the dark stairway.

"I'll go first," Johnny offered.

When they found the right door, Johnny knocked softly. "I hate to wake the baby," he whispered.

When no one came, he knocked again, a little bit louder.

Finally, they heard the sound of shuffling feet, and the door opened. "Hello," Papa said sleepily.

Grace hung back, and there was no rush for hugs. Papa's face seemed tired and drawn. He stepped aside and lifted a hand to welcome them in.

"Mr. McFarland, I'm Louise Showalter," Miss Louise said, extending one of her gloved hands for Papa to shake. "This is my husband, Johnny."

Johnny nodded, since both of his hands were under the turkey.

"We brought you some dinner," Miss Louise said brightly.

"I see," said Papa. "Well, we can certainly use it."

"Hi, Papa," Grace said.

He tried to smile. He really did try. But "Grace" was all he said.

She handed him the pie.

At first Grace didn't understand why Papa wasn't happier to see her. Was he disappointed that she hadn't stayed at the mission to watch over Iggy and Owen? But once inside the apartment, Grace understood why her father seemed so sad. The place was awful. Worst of all was how dark it was. There wasn't a single window—not one. The only light came from a kerosene lantern set on an upturned orange crate.

Grace's eyes flicked around. She saw a small sink and refrigerator at one end of the room, and a gas ring with just one burner on the floor for cooking. But there was no table on which to eat, no chairs to sit on either. And the cold cement floor was dirty, and without a rug.

"The furniture . . ." Papa began. "A friend of mine said he'd give us a couple chairs tomorrow. I'm sorry there's no place to sit."

"Well, let me put this turkey over here," Johnny said, placing it on the drain board near the sink.

Suddenly, there was a tiny baby noise, and Grace saw movement in the opposite corner of the room.

"Mama!" she exclaimed, rushing to kneel beside her mother, who lay curled up, with the baby tucked in her arms, on a mattress on the floor. A single blanket covered her.

She smiled up at Grace. "How are you, darlin'?"

Grace knelt to give her a hug, and Mama kissed her on the cheek.

"Good. I'm good! I'm staying with some nice people." She glanced behind her. "Miss Louise and Mr. Johnny and their family. They're taking good care of me. And look—" Grace stood the new doll up on the edge of the mattress. "I got this doll for Christmas."

"Ah, she's pretty, Grace. Have you named her yet?"

Grace started to shake her head but then quickly decided. "Ruth!" she announced.

Mama grinned. "You wouldn't be naming that doll for me, would you?"

"I *like* the name!" Grace said.

Mama smiled again, but there was not much sparkle in her sad, tired eyes. Grace pressed her lips together.

"Would you like to see the baby?" Mama asked.

Grace nodded eagerly, and Mama pulled the blanket down to reveal a tiny, scrunched-up face with a little puckered mouth.

"Baby Holly," Grace said softly. Carefully, she touched one of the baby's miniature fingers.

Behind her, all was quiet. Miss Louise and Johnny waited in the kitchen part of the room with Papa, who stood with his hands in his pockets.

"Are you hungry? Can we fix you some dinner with what we've brought?" Miss Louise asked.

Papa didn't answer, so Mama did. "Thank you," she said. "Clement and I will be fine. We'll eat in a bit. The turkey smells wonderful."

"There's apple pie, too, Mama," Grace pointed out. "And pickles and green beans and rolls—and some fudge—and cookies that I decorated. Oh, and we brought a gift for Holly— a little pink sweater. It's *so* cute!"

"It sounds wonderful," Mama said. She looked up at Miss Louise and Johnny. "I can't thank you enough."

Johnny fumbled with his gloves. "We could probably get you a table."

"If someone has one they don't need," Mama said.

"We'd be obliged," Papa added.

"How about some dishes? For cooking?" Miss Louise inquired.

Papa barely nodded.

"Will you be here—long?" Johnny asked.

Papa shrugged and sighed. "Long as I can pay the rent.

Been gettin' a little relief money, but there's been no work, not for some time."

"It's awful," Johnny sympathized. "My father, out in Kansas, had to sell his farm this year. He and my mother moved in with my oldest brother."

There was a pause, and no one said anything.

"Mr. McFarland," Miss Louise began, "please know that we'll take good care of Grace for you. She's a dear and no trouble to us. No trouble at all. It's the least we can do."

"If you ever want to talk with her, just call," Johnny added. "I'll leave the number." He scribbled on a piece of paper. "It's Metropolitan 7772."

Papa smiled halfway. "Don't have no phone here."

Johnny handed him the number. "But if you can get to a phone."

"Clement, take it," Mama said from her corner.

Grace suddenly jumped to her feet. "Papa!" she exclaimed. "Your fiddle!"

Papa smiled for the first time. "Can you believe it? Good ole Ferguson picked it up out of the pile on the street and brung it to us at Stewart's."

Grace swung around to face Johnny and Miss Louise. "You should hear Papa play! He and Mr. Ferguson were the hit of the neighborhood."

"Say, we'd love to hear you sometime," Johnny told him.

"Acch." Papa cast his eyes down and stuffed his hands even deeper into his pockets. "Ain't much in the mood for music these days."

"No," Miss Louise agreed sympathetically. "I don't imagine so."

Johnny shuffled his feet. "Well, then. We probably ought to be going."

"Yes, we should," Miss Louise agreed.

Grace returned to kneel by her mother and felt a deep ache in her chest. She didn't want to leave Mama and her tiny new sister in a cold, dark room with no windows. She remembered the diamond brooch she still had in her cigar box. "I have a present for you, Mama," she whispered. "I don't have it *now*, with me, but I'll bring it . . . maybe next time."

"Don't you be worryin' about presents for me," Mama told her. "I'll be okay." She squeezed Grace's hand. "You just take care of yourself. And mind your manners, Grace. Be the good girl I know you are."

"I will," Grace promised.

On her way out, Grace stopped at the door beside her father and looked up at him. "Are you mad, Papa? Are you mad because I didn't stay at the mission to watch Iggy and Owen?"

Papa pulled his hands out of his pockets, knelt beside her, and took her arms. "Oh no, Grace. I'm not angry. I'm very grateful you had a family to take you in. Iggy—he went home with some good folks, too, the way you did. And Miss Claiborne tells me Owen has friends he won't be parted from—that he went to the moving-picture show. The boys are all right. Don't worry."

Grace swallowed. "But what about Pete?" she asked. "How's Pete?"

Papa dropped his eyes. His grip on Grace loosened and his voice broke. "We are praying for him, Grace."

All the way home in the car, Grace sat silently, shrouded in worry. Mama and Papa's situation was much worse than she had imagined. In the front seat, Miss Louise and Johnny were quiet, too. When they returned to the Hammonds' house, Grace dashed upstairs to change into her old green dress from the mission. She was glad Mama hadn't seen the fancy new clothes beneath her coat.

Sitting on her bed, Grace crossed her arms and held her elbows. The new doll stared up at her from where it had been dropped on the rug. In her mind all Grace could see was a dark room and Mama huddled with the baby. And all she could hear was Papa's voice, breaking, over and over. *We are praying for him, Grace.*

When Miss Louise came into the room, Grace didn't move.

"I'm sorry," Miss Louise said, sitting beside Grace and putting an arm around her shoulders. "I'm sorry for what has happened to your family. So many people are struggling to survive right now. It's not just your parents, Grace."

"I know," Grace said sadly. "I know they're not the only ones." But knowing that was little consolation.

Miss Louise squeezed Grace's shoulder. "Johnny and I would never . . . well, we want you to know that you can stay with us for as long as you'd like."

Grace knew what Miss Louise couldn't bring herself to say: that they could never send her back to live in a pitiful place like that. And no, Grace thought, she would never *want* to live in a place like that! What would they sit on? How would they eat? Where would they sleep?

You can stay with us for as long as you'd like. . . .

Maybe it was true, what Esterbelle had said. Maybe Miss Louise and Johnny *did* want to adopt her. If Grace wanted to be adopted . . .

Her eyes blurred with tears, because suddenly it stood there and it was wonderful and scary at the same time—this enormous possibility, this incredible thing that could save her from a life of hunger and unknown days in a dreary, dark basement room with no windows.

Was this the day of reckoning Reverend Saunders talked about? Was this the new life the Ouija board had predicted?

But how could she? What about Pete? She could never leave Pete.

We are praying for him, Grace. . . .

When Miss Louise put an arm around her, Grace closed her eyes, not wanting to think about it, not wanting to imagine how she would ever decide if she were given the choice.

THE SIGN FOR *FRIEND*

Winter, cold," Grace repeated, making two fists and moving them in and out quickly, as though shivering.

Joanna grinned her approval. Every day, she had been teaching Grace how to express more words in American Sign Language: *want, hungry, cake, tired, sleep, understand.*

Lots of the words were easy to remember, Grace found. *Think* was tapping the forehead with an index finger. *Baby* was rocking a pretend one in your arms. And the sign for *friend* was the two index fingers hooked together.

A snowstorm blanketed Washington, D.C., in the week following Christmas. The two girls and Miss Louise spent hours together, sharing lessons in sign language and knitting. Miss Louise bought Grace some pink yarn so she could make a baby blanket for Holly, taught Grace the top hand of "Silent Night" on the piano, and gave her some lined stationery and envelopes so that she could write to Pete. Joanna showed her how to watercolor and taught her to play whist.

When Miss Louise was busy ironing or giving herself an egg shampoo, the two girls never ran out of things to do. They giggled over the newspaper comics, especially *The Gumps* and *Little Mary Mixup*. With frequent taste testing, they made gingerbread. And together they listened, Joanna with her hand on the radio, the night Miss Betsy sang with Three Maids and a Mike. "Hooray!" they cheered after Miss Betsy's flawless performance.

Other times they simply sat on the window seat in the hall upstairs, watching the snow fall and transform the yards along Connecticut Avenue into winter wonderlands with huge, fluffy drifts. It was there, on the window seat late one afternoon, while Grace worked on a letter to Pete, that Joanna wrote and handed Grace a note: *When I go tutor, you come. Ride trolley home. Stop hospital and see Pete. A secret.*

Grace looked up at her. "But I'm afraid they won't let us in."

Joanna shook her head, took back the note, and wrote quickly beneath the other words: *We say we not touch. Short visit.*

"But what about your tutor's son? Doesn't he take you home?" Grace asked.

Joanna continued writing. *Say we old enough. Go ourselves.*

The idea excited Grace, although she was still doubtful they could pull it off. "Do you mean it, Joanna? We can go see Pete?"

Joanna watched her carefully and understood the spoken questions. Smiling, she made two fists and swept them forward, the sign for *try*.

When the snow finally stopped and the roads were plowed, Johnny and Grace delivered a small table, as well as blankets, more food, and a skillet to Grace's parents. Not much had changed. There was a small rug on the floor and Aunt Emma had sent dishes. But the room was still dark and smelled foul besides because of the mushroom boxes Papa had bought.

"Guy says I can make me twenty dollars a month growing these things," Papa told Johnny.

Grace held her nose and studied the long, shallow boxes of rich, black dirt, but she couldn't see any mushrooms growing.

"It's the manure what makes 'em smell so bad," Papa explained.

Mama had a terrible cold, and Holly cried the whole time. "Don't come near," Mama warned, putting up a hand. "I'm loaded with bad germs."

Grace stood back, frustrated that she couldn't get near Mama and the baby. "I wrote a letter to Pete," she told her mother loudly, so Mama could hear above the baby's crying. "Miss Louise mailed it for me, but he hasn't written back yet."

Mama sneezed.

"Has he written to you?" Grace asked.

"No." Mama sniffed. "It's probably difficult—" She covered her mouth to sneeze again.

"How about Iggy and Owen?" Grace asked.

"What? . . . Shush, Holly, I can't hear." Mama tried to quiet the baby. "I'm sorry, Grace. This cold . . ." And Holly cried even harder.

"Here, Mama, here's another hankie," Grace said, offering the clean one she had in her own pocket. It was obvious that Mama just needed to rest. Grace was disappointed; she had wanted to tell her mother about the piano and about the pink blanket she was knitting, and the watercolor lessons from Joanna. But it didn't seem like the right time.

After her mother took the handkerchief, Grace walked over to stand beside Johnny and wait for him to finish talking to Papa. It was cold in the apartment. Grace suddenly realized she had never even taken her coat off. It's no wonder Mama had a cold, she thought. She hoped the baby didn't get sick, too. She peered around at the dark, damp apartment and could not imagine living in it. Just the thought made her anxious, and eager to leave.

Gently, she pulled on Johnny's coat sleeve. "Don't forget," she said, "we need to stop at the drugstore for some Harper's remedy."

"You're right," Johnny said. "Louise has had a sore throat and a headache all day. I guess we need to be getting home."

Papa stared at his mushroom boxes and kept shaking his head. "I'm sure they'll sprout anytime now. Guy says it'll take a few days, though."

Johnny and Grace looked at each other.

"Bye, Papa," Grace said. But Papa didn't turn around as they left, closing the door behind them.

Back at the Hammonds' house, where it was warm and the smell of a simmering pot roast greeted them, Grace hung her coat in the front closet and asked if she could be the one to take Miss Louise the warm lemon juice and honey that Johnny said would be good for her throat.

When the snow finally began to melt, Esterbelle and her mother returned from Virginia. It was a busy time in the house. While the Hammonds bustled about preparing for a New Year's Eve bridge party, Miss Betsy had a telephone call offering her a full-time singing job in New York City.

"They want me up there the day after tomorrow!" she exclaimed.

Everyone was happy for her. Mr. Hammond kept saying it was the "big break" Betsy had been waiting for, and Mrs. Hammond said she would bake a cake to celebrate. When it was finished, Miss Louise decorated the cake with a musical staff made from strings of licorice and notes created with chocolates.

"Can you imagine?" Miss Louise asked Grace as she put the finishing touches on the cake. "Singing in a nightclub with famous bands?"

"I'd be too scared," Grace said, dipping her finger into the frosting bowl for a sample.

Joanna, sitting beside Grace at the kitchen table, did the same.

"So, have you girls written down any New Year's resolutions?" Miss Louise asked.

Joanna replied by finger spelling. "Be more patient," she said. "Even people I not like."

Grace giggled. She knew Joanna was referring to Esterbelle.

"What about you, Grace?" Miss Louise asked.

Grace bit her lip and pulled on the end of one braid, thinking.

"You don't have to say it out loud," Miss Louise said, seeing that Grace was having a hard time. "It can be something you promise yourself."

Then Grace knew instantly what she *would* resolve: to put Miss Betsy's pin back in her jewelry box once and for all, and vow never to steal again. Grace knew in her heart it was wrong to have taken it. What had stopped her from replacing it thus far was that she kept thinking that if anything happened—if she was sent back to the mission, or returned home—then *at least* she would have that pin for Mama. And if things were bad—*really* bad—then that pin could help get them what they needed, whether it was medicine or milk or a loaf of bread.

Joanna was knocking on the kitchen table to get Miss Louise's attention.

"Me?" Miss Louise asked. "What's *my* resolution?"

Grace was glad for the excuse not to think about hers. "Yes!" she joined in eagerly. "What's yours, Miss Louise?"

Miss Louise put the frosting knife in the bowl, pressed her lips together, and slowly wiped her hands on a dish towel, thinking. "I want to be happy," she said, signing at the same time. "I want everyone in this family to be happy."

The sign for *happy* was to place both hands, palms facing you, on the chest, then move the hands up, brushing the chest and making a circular motion twice before resting the hands again on the chest. Grace hadn't known the sign. Now she would never forget the motion: touch the heart, and lift it.

After the cake was placed on a crystal cake pedestal on the dining-room sideboard, Grace, Esterbelle, and Joanna went to work wrapping ashtrays and packs of fancy napkins to use as bridge prizes. They also set the tables with cardboard hats crowned 1933 and paper horns filled with confetti.

Then that evening, while the adults played cards, the girls took their slices of cake into the parlor, where they sat on the rug cutting out paper dolls and listening to mystery stories on the radio. A week away seemed to have softened Esterbelle, if only by a hair. She shared a can of jumbo peanuts she had brought back from Virginia and confided that the trip had been boring. But when Grace and Joanna signed to each other, Esterbelle complained.

"It's not fair. You're leaving me out," Esterbelle accused.

"We're just talking," Grace said, shrugging.

"You're not either!" Esterbelle objected, scooping up her peanuts as she left and demonstrating that, really, she hadn't changed a whit.

Despite the late night, everyone was up early the next morning to say good-bye to Miss Betsy, whose packed belongings filled the front hallway. Grace fingered the string handle of a hatbox set on top of a trunk and thought somberly how the house wouldn't be the same without Miss Betsy's exuberance. Even if her leaving did mean that Grace would have a whole room to herself. "Hey! You can move into that big brass bed tonight," Miss Betsy had told her with a wink.

Although Grace loved her little rollaway bed, she was certain she could adjust to a big bed of her own. But that night as Grace plumped the oversized pillows, a terrible realization hit her: Miss Betsy had taken all her things, including her jewelry box—and Grace had never replaced the diamond brooch!

She slumped back against the pillows, disappointed in herself. Maybe, she hoped, Miss Betsy would be so busy and so happy with her new job in New York City that she would never miss the pin. Or perhaps Grace could plant it somewhere and make it look as though the pin had fallen behind the bureau—or beneath the bed. Pulling up the soft quilts, Grace snuggled into the brass bed, confident she could think of *something*.

She closed her eyes to sleep and, as she did every night, prayed God to bless everyone in her family: Iggy and Owen and Mama curled up with Holly. Poor Papa—was he still fretting over his mushrooms? And finally Pete. Grace found it difficult to picture Pete. Did he have a room to himself? Did nurses bring him everything he wanted? What was happening to Pete?

All of her brothers and her sister were in different places now, she realized. Not even two of them were together anymore. She kept her hands, already folded in prayer, beneath her chin and for a long time lay quietly, staring into the darkness and wondering what would happen to them all.

Days slid by quickly after the holidays. There was a trip to the zoo to sled down the hills and two more shopping trips to prepare Grace for school. So many new dresses joined the ones hanging in her closet that Grace had to push the green dress from the mission all the way to the back in order to make room.

Soon, Miss Louise returned to work, too, and a new routine began. One bright, cold January morning, Grace found herself standing before a sixth-grade class at nearby Oyster Grammar School.

"Let's welcome Grace McFarland," said the teacher, Miss Fawcett, who was plump and wore reading glasses perched halfway down her nose. Although she had a stern look, Miss Fawcett was kind and spoke in a gentle, unrushed voice. "Why don't you sit here, dear," she said, placing Grace at a small wooden desk carved over the years with initials and nicknames. Grace was also given a set of books and a pen, which she filled with ink at the teacher's desk.

The cookie monitor, a boy named Rommy, handed Grace an extra graham cracker on her first day of school. And at recess a girl named Beverly came over to the monkey bars where Grace stood alone and invited her to play dodgeball. "I was new last year," Beverly told her.

When it was time for lunch, Grace met Mrs. Hammond out front and walked home for a bowl of tomato soup, then returned to school for the afternoon.

Meanwhile, Esterbelle went to a private girls' school, while Joanna, who had caught a cold and was confined to bed with a mustard plaster on her chest, had her lessons at home with her mother, as she always did. By the end of the week, Grace was allowed to visit Joanna, provided she sat at the far end of the bed.

"I got a letter from Pete today!" Grace told her, holding up the small white envelope that had welcomed her arrival home from school.

"What he say?" Joanna asked in sign as she sat up against her pillows. Her blond hair was pinned back behind her ears, and with the smelly mustard plaster gone, she wore a pretty blue satin bed jacket that Grace admired.

"Here—you can read it," Grace said, handing Joanna the letter.

Grace walked over to stand beside her, even though she wasn't supposed to be that close, and read the letter again over Joanna's shoulder.

Dear Grace,

Thank you for writing and telling me all about the Hammonds and the boardinghouse. It sounds great. Well, except for that girl Esterbelle. I'm glad you got to see Holly. Papa wrote me about the baby and the new apartment. The new place sounds awful, but I guess you've seen it so you must know.

A woman named Miss Adelle is writing this for me. She's a nurse who has been very kind to me. She brought me a book last week, but I'm too weak to read it. The cough is bad. You ask if I have my own room. I'm not in a room at all, but in the hallway it's so crowded. The good thing is I'm under a small window. When I look up, I can see a patch of blue sky and part of a tree branch. Right now I can see a sparrow looking in at me.

I think about you, Grace. I think of all the fun we had together, you and me. You're the best sister anyone could ever have.

Please write again.

Love,

Pete

"Nice letter," Joanna said in sign.

"Nice. Yes," Grace agreed. She took the letter and, as she walked back toward the end of the bed, tucked it into the pocket of her dress. She was happy to have it, although it hurt to think of Pete lying in a hallway, staring up at a tiny patch of sky.

Joanna seemed to sense Grace's worry. She was an expert at reading Grace's moods. She patted the bed. "How was school?" she asked in sign.

Grace brightened, because she loved her new school. "I wish you could come with me," she said slowly and clearly, hoping Joanna could read her lips.

"I went school," Joanna said with a combination of sign and finger spelling. "Children mean. Call me names because I not hear."

This didn't surprise her; Grace knew how cruel other children could be.

Frustrated that finger spelling took so long, Joanna pulled out a pad of paper and wrote. *I not allowed use sign in school. Only read lips. Teacher is man with mustache. I not see his lips. He think I retarded. Tell my parents—take me home.*

"I would never *want* to go to school after that!" Grace sympathized.

Joanna reached forward to touch Grace's hand. "But I want go school. School for deaf." Two fingers near her left ear for *deaf.* "Father say no. Better be with hearing." Joanna's shoulders slumped. "Not better." She shook her head sadly and held her right index finger up in front of her mouth and made a small circle, the sign for *lonely.*

Lonely, yes. Grace nodded. She knew how much Joanna longed to be part of the world.

Joanna tapped Grace's hand again. "We plan trip visit Pete."

And they did. They planned their secret trip. Assuming Joanna was all better by Saturday, they decided to make their visit then, after Joanna's tutoring session.

"What are you talking about?" Esterbelle suddenly asked from the doorway.

Her voice startled Grace. "Oh, I was just telling Joanna about the Lone Ranger," Grace lied. "Remember that radio show we heard last week?"

"I don't believe you," Esterbelle said. "You're up to something, I can tell."

Joanna and Grace grinned at each other. They couldn't help it.

"You'll be sorry. I'll find out and you'll be sorry!" Esterbelle warned, turning on her heel.

Joanna boldly stuck out her tongue, and Grace rolled her eyes as Esterbelle stormed away.

But at dinner Friday night, there was Big Trouble, just as Esterbelle had promised.

CONFESSIONS

Grace knew something was up the minute Esterbelle grinned at her from across the dining-room table.

"Mother and I are inviting you to my tap-dance recital tomorrow," Esterbelle told Grace in her sweetest, most syrupy voice. Then she turned to Miss Louise. "Of course, she'll have to dress up," she instructed. "Everyone has to dress up. Afterward Mother's taking us for a Lucky Monday." She turned back to Grace, who had stopped eating. "It's root beer with vanilla ice cream. I'll bet you never had one."

Grace flashed a frightened look at Joanna across the table. Tomorrow was their visit to Pete.

But Miss Louise didn't know about their secret plans. She smiled her approval at Esterbelle. "What a nice offer," she said. "Grace would love it."

"No, I wouldn't!" Grace protested. "I mean that I can't—because I promised Joanna I would go with her to her tutor."

Esterbelle narrowed her eyes.

"You can go with Joanna another time," Miss Louise told Grace.

"But I *want* to go with Joanna," Grace insisted. She paused. "I would *rather* go with Joanna."

Angry, Esterbelle crossed her arms.

"Grace, it'll be tiring, just waiting for Joanna to finish," Mrs. Hammond added from the far end of the table. "You'll be bored."

"No, I won't!" Grace insisted. "I'll take a book and read."

Esterbelle uncrossed her arms and turned to Miss Louise. "It's fine with me if Grace doesn't want to go to my recital. She probably has *other plans* with Joanna—like visiting the pawnshop!"

Grace's mouth dropped open.

"I didn't want to say anything," Esterbelle went on, "but, Miss Louise, you should know that Grace is a thief. She took a diamond pin from Miss Betsy's jewelry box!"

Grace's eyes flashed. She stood, scraping back her chair and balling up her fists. "Well, at least I have a father, Esterbelle Scarlotti! At least my father didn't run off with a gypsy!"

Mrs. Hammond gasped.

Mrs. Scarlotti slapped a hand on her chest. "Good Lord!" she cried.

"Grace, what on earth are you talking about?" Miss Louise was startled by the outburst, too. "Esterbelle's father didn't run away. He's out west working on the Hoover Dam. He was here at Thanksgiving—he ate with us!"

Esterbelle wrinkled her nose and sneered at Grace, and Grace realized instantly that she had been tricked. Esterbelle had lied to get Grace to confide a secret, fully intending to use it against her one day.

"Grace is not the *only* one with a secret!" Esterbelle added. "Joanna has a secret, too. She's got a journal, and one day, well, I didn't mean to, but—"

Esterbelle was *not* going to get away with this. Quickly, Grace picked up her glass and flung the milk across the table into Esterbelle's face.

"Ohhhhhhhhhh!" Esterbelle screamed, wiping the milk out of her eyes and seeing with horror how it dripped down the front of her dress.

"Good heavens!" Mrs. Scarlotti cried.

"Grace McFarland! To your room!" Miss Louise ordered.

Grace was so angry, her cheeks grew hot and her fists clenched tightly as she stood by her bed. "Esterbelle lied to me. She made me trade secrets!"

"Calm down," Miss Louise said.

"She sneaks around, listening to people's conversations. She doesn't care about anyone's privacy. Look what she did! She read Joanna's journal!"

Miss Louise nodded, put both hands on Grace's shoulders, and made her sit on the edge of her bed.

Grace tried to take a deep breath, but she was too angry to calm down. Plus she was worried that now Miss Louise would ask Miss Betsy about the brooch and they'd find out it was missing. Grace frowned and chewed on her bottom lip. She had meant to put back the pin.

"Esterbelle is mean. She tricked me!" Grace said, jumping up and stomping her foot.

Miss Louise did not seem very angry. "I always had a feeling Esterbelle was jealous of you," she said.

"She's not jealous, she's evil! And she *hates* me!"

"No," Miss Louise said, shaking her head. "She's not evil, Grace. And she doesn't hate you. She's jealous, that's all."

"Of *what?*" Grace threw up her hands.

Miss Louise patted the bed and made Grace sit down again.

"For one thing," Miss Louise began, "she's jealous because Joanna likes *you* and not her. Not only that, but Esterbelle resents anyone who upstages her. She used to live a very privileged life up in Philadelphia with her chauffeur and her maids. But when the stock market crashed, the family lost everything. Mr. Scarlotti went to work on the dam. Mrs. Scarlotti and Esterbelle came here, to be near relatives."

Grace turned to Miss Louise. "But Esterbelle takes dancing lessons!"

"Yes. Her grandmother does send them money," Miss Louise explained.

"And she's jealous of my new clothes—even though she has lots of nice dresses herself!"

"What Esterbelle doesn't realize—what I hope you'll remember, Grace—is that all your life there will be people who have more than you—and people who have less."

Grace hung her head.

"What's *really* important," Miss Louise went on to say, "are the connections you have with the people you love. Your family, your friends, Grace—truly, those are the things that matter. Those are the things that will always matter the most."

Family. Grace stared into her lap. All of this seemed so silly compared to what her family faced. Mama and Papa, hungry, in a cold, dark room with stinky dirt. Owen and Iggy split up. Pete so weak he couldn't write.

When Grace looked up, she was surprised to see Miss Louise's eyes moist with tears.

"I'm so sorry, Miss Louise!" Grace apologized. "I embarrassed you. I should never have done that!"

"No, Grace. It's not because of what you did." She put a handkerchief to her eyes. "I was thinking of my own family. The baby I lost. It's left such a hole. . . . I've never been able to fill it."

"But you have me!" Grace blurted.

Miss Louise looked up at her. "Oh, I do wish I had you," she said, dropping her hands into her lap. "More than anything else in the world I wish I had a nice little girl like you."

"But you do!" Grace insisted. "And I'd do anything to make you happy, Miss Louise."

Miss Louise took Grace's hand. "Do you mean that?" she asked.

"Of course I mean it," Grace assured her.

Miss Louise cleared her throat. "Grace, I . . . you know I'm so sorry for your family's misfortune. It's no fault of theirs. But we *can* help. We've been meaning to ask you, Johnny and I, if you would like to . . . I mean, that Johnny and I, we would love to adopt you and give you a proper home."

Grace dropped her eyes because she didn't know what to say right off. Of course she would rather live at the Hammonds' than in that terrible subbasement. Who wouldn't? But how could she leave her family? Tears pooled in her eyes, too.

"Oh, Grace, I'm so sorry. I shouldn't have—"

"No!" Grace stopped her. She didn't want Miss Louise to take back the offer. "I don't ever want to live in that horrible basement! And I don't want to change stinky diapers anymore! Or be hungry!"

"Grace, please, you need to think about it, dear. Don't give us your answer right now."

Miss Louise's voice was *so* kind that Grace suddenly felt terrible. *Terrible* because she knew she wasn't the nice little girl Miss Louise deserved. "I'm *not* a very good person, Miss Louise. You need to know that."

"Don't be silly—"

Grace shook her head. "No. No, it's true. I am everything Esterbelle said I was!"

Quickly, Grace retrieved the cigar box from underneath the rollaway bed and thrust it into Miss Louise's hands. "Go ahead. Open it!"

Slowly, Miss Lousie opened the lid. For a moment she sat, silently staring at the jumble of odds and ends: the bag of marbles, the oyster shell, the cuckoo bird from Grandma Rosa's clock, a folded napkin that contained a very stale biscuit. On top of it all was the gold star napkin ring from the tearoom at Woodward and Lothrop. And beside it, Miss Betsy's glittering diamond pin.

When Miss Louise pressed her lips together, Grace felt her heart drop. "My brother warned me I was going to turn into a thief," she said, "and I guess it happened. I knew I should have put that pin back. All along I knew it. And I meant to. . . . *Honest!*" She paused and her voice softened. "But I never did."

Miss Louise picked up the pin, and for a moment neither one spoke.

"I was going to give it to Mama," Grace said.

"Your mother?" Miss Louise seemed surprised.

Grace nodded. "My mother never had anything as fancy as that pin. Mama never even had a diamond wedding ring like you, Miss Louise. She had a little band, a little gold band; but she lost it doing the wash once. We never could find it. Mama was heartbroke. And I know that's no excuse. But I don't know what to say, except that I'm sorry. Guess I'm just no good. I'm no better than Esterbelle and what she done."

Miss Louise did not agree. "No," she said with a sigh. "You're not a thief, Grace."

Grace wiped her nose. "I'm not?"

Miss Louise shook her head. "If you were truly a thief, Grace, you wouldn't be handing me this box."

But Grace didn't understand, and frowned.

"I think that you're a little girl who has known what it's like to be truly hungry and cold," Miss Louise went on. "A little girl who has had to do some extraordinary things to stay alive in this world."

Holding the pin, Miss Louise closed the cigar box and handed the box back to Grace. "Here," she said. "Miss Betsy has her pin back now. We will never hold it against you."

"You won't?" Grace asked.

"No. We all make mistakes, Grace. We all do things we're

sorry for later. The important thing is to admit it, and make amends."

Relieved by Miss Louise's reaction, Grace sat down beside her on the bed again and after a time said quietly, "I'll bet you never did anything as bad as me."

Deep in her own thoughts, Miss Louise ran her thumb over the pin in her hand. "One of the worst things I ever did," she began, "was invite a little girl home from the mission knowing full well she had a family. My motive was selfish, Grace. I wanted a little girl of my own. I thought if I made her comfortable enough she would choose to stay. I knew her family situation was desperate. But I didn't think enough about what it might do to that child, or to her family."

Grace knew that Miss Louise was talking about her.

"I'm still glad, though," Grace said gently. "I'm still glad you came and got me."

"That's not all," Miss Louise continued. "You should know that one reason we took you to see your parents so soon after Christmas is that we knew the apartment was awful. We wanted you to see where you would live if you went home."

Miss Louise stopped speaking, and Grace felt something shift between them.

"Everybody told me to adopt a baby. It would be so much easier, they said. But they didn't know just how painful that would have been for me." Miss Louise lifted her chin. "No, I could never love another baby. An older child would be better, I thought. Then we found you, Grace. When I saw you in the mission, I said to myself, 'That's what my little girl would look like now.'"

Miss Louise dropped her head again, and Grace could feel the heaviness that had settled upon her. "Miss Louise," she said, frantically searching her mind for something to say. "What was your little girl's name?"

When Miss Louise turned to her, Grace wasn't sure she would answer or not—and she worried she had just made things even worse.

But Miss Louise replied with a slight lift in her voice, "Her name was Iris."

Grace started to smile. "Iris," she repeated. "It's a pretty name. It's a pretty flower."

"Yes," Miss Louise agreed, "she was a pretty little flower."

Tears were gathering in Miss Louise's eyes again. Grace reached over to take her hand, and, quickly, Miss Louise composed herself. She squeezed Grace's fingers and let go. "There," she said. "We've both been honest, haven't we? You see, we've both made mistakes."

Grace nodded, but she wasn't sure what Miss Louise meant by that last statement. About both of them making mistakes.

When Miss Louise smiled bravely, Grace did, too.

"Now, there is this other matter of flying milk," Miss Louise said. "I hate to punish you, Grace—"

"Oh, but you have to, Miss Louise! I did a *terrible* thing throwing that milk at Esterbelle. You need to punish me. You should make me write a letter of apology—and forbid me to play with Esterbelle!"

"Would that be punishment, Grace?" Miss Louise asked.

"Well, not exactly," Grace had to admit with a sheepish grin.

Miss Louise reached over to pat Grace's leg. "Why don't

you write a note of apology," she suggested. "And I suppose you'll have to stay in your room the rest of the evening. Do you have a book to read?"

"Yes, ma'am," Grace said.

Then all at once, Miss Louise got up and left the room, taking the diamond brooch and quietly closing the door behind her.

Still holding her cigar box, Grace remained seated on the bed. She was darn lucky she wasn't being packed off right this minute for what she'd done, she thought. And she was glad she had confessed. She hoped Miss Louise was right, that if Grace *really* were a thief she'd have hidden that pin under her mattress—or sold it by now!

Miss Louise had said she wouldn't hold anything against her.

Grace stared at the closed door.

But did that mean Miss Louise still wanted her to stay?

A DESPERATE ATTEMPT

R ain pounded the roof and rattled the drain spouts the next morning. Grace was disappointed that Miss Louise had gone shopping already and hadn't even said good-bye.

When the egg man came to the back door, dripping wet, and complained about the slippery streets, Grace felt her spirits lift a little. She was sure Mrs. Hammond would forbid Joanna to keep her appointment with the tutor, and then Grace would at least have her at the house for company.

But Joanna was resolute. "We be fine," she insisted with strong sign. "We take care ourselves." She pulled on Grace's hands. "Come," she signed.

Mrs. Hammond turned to Grace. "It's okay," the older woman said, unable to resist a slight smile. "As long as you've written your note to Esterbelle, you may go."

Grace had not expected this. Was it possible she'd be seeing Pete after all?

By early afternoon, Grace sat alone in the living room of Mrs. Viola Spence with *Little Women* on her lap, listening as

Joanna in the next room began her tutoring session in lipreading—and speech.

Grace was intrigued because she had never heard Joanna speak before.

"Sit. Set. Sat," Joanna's strange, unsteady voice repeated.

"Good!" Mrs. Spence declared. "The next three."

"Suit. Sight. Say."

Grace pulled the chain under the fringed lamp shade beside her, flooding her lap with light, and opened to page one. But she had too many things to think about. Did Miss Louise still want to adopt her? Grace worried that she had changed her mind. . . . And what if she hadn't? What would Pete say? Grace had some gingersnaps wrapped up in a napkin and Pete's bag of marbles, which she was going to give back to him—for good luck.

Closing her book, Grace listened to the speech lessons and wondered why Joanna never spoke at home. Was she afraid?

Raindrops streaked down the windows and thumped on the metal garbage cans at the side of the house. Grace took a sip of the hot tea with lemon that Mrs. Spence had made for her in a flowered teacup. Miss Louise needed Grace as much as Grace needed her. In God's eyes, wouldn't it be okay, then, to let herself be adopted?

But what about Mama? Would she let Grace go? Would she miss Grace even though she had Holly now?

And how would she ever explain it to Iggy and Owen? Grace loved them both so much. Her expression, melting into melancholy, brightened suddenly when it dawned on her that

Miss Louise would surely let the boys visit. Miss Louise would be tickled at the things they did—the things they said! Joanna would adore the boys, too. They would all have such a good time, baking cookies, going to the zoo, playing hide-and-seek.

Reassured, Grace stirred her tea again and casually examined the silver spoon in her hand. *Sterling*, she saw written in tiny letters. Pete told her once that sterling silver was always worth something because it could be melted down and made into other things. Grace rested the spoon in the saucer and sighed, relieved that there would be no more stealing. No more "borrowing." Not ever. Not even if she returned home.

Setting her book down, Grace got up to walk around the room and, through a crack in the door, could see Joanna sitting at a desk across from her tutor. A candle was lit between them.

"Pay. *Pie*," Joanna said, blowing out the candle on the second *P* word.

"Very good," Mrs. Spence said, relighting the candle. "Again."

When the lesson was over, the girls pulled on galoshes, scooped up their books and the umbrella, and ran to catch the trolley. After paying the fare, they took seats up front and sat quietly while the noisy trolley rolled on its tracks down a long hill. Joanna kept her hands folded over the little purse in her lap, and Grace wondered if she was nervous about going to the Tuberculosis Hospital.

"Your voice sounds nice," Grace spelled out with her fingers.

Joanna blushed and then pointed to herself, making the sign for *remember*. She paused, then made the sign for *hear* by bouncing her index finger against her ear. But when she saw Grace's confusion, she pulled out a pad of paper from her purse and began writing: *I remember some sounds. Sound of bells. Sound of rooster crow. Sound of my name.*

They had never talked about Joanna's deafness, how it had happened. Grace knew only what Miss Louise had told her, that Joanna was four when she became sick with scarlet fever and lost her hearing. It never occurred to Grace that Joanna might actually remember how some things sounded.

Joanna took the pad back from Grace and continued to write: *Thank you for last night. For stop Esterbelle talk about me.*

Grace laughed. "Can you believe I did that?"

Joanna recalled the dripping milk by making a face and wiping her hands down the front of her coat.

"She deserved it!" Grace said.

Suddenly, Joanna was urging Grace to get up. The next stop was theirs.

The rain had stopped, and the girls didn't need the umbrella as they walked along the wet sidewalk, Grace avoiding the cracks because it was bad luck to step on one. After three blocks they turned the corner onto Thirteenth Street, and Joanna pointed to a huge brick building on a hill.

"That's the Tuberculosis Hospital?" Grace asked. She wondered how they would ever find Pete inside such a big place. She rehearsed in her head what she would say to the receptionist. *My name is Grace McFarland. This is Joanna Hammond. We're here to deliver a gift to one of the patients, Peter McFarland. We won't be long and we won't touch anything.*

But there was no one in the hospital lobby when they came through the door. The girls looked at each other. Could it possibly be that easy? Grace and Joanna kept walking.

Right away the air smelled stuffy and stale. Grace heard someone coughing. But when she stopped to listen, she realized it was the sound of many people coughing, their harsh, hacking sounds echoing down the dull, gray-painted corridor. Grace panicked a little, but decided there was no point in telling Joanna how awful it sounded. It would only scare her. Instead, she took Joanna's hand and proceeded.

Joanna's eyes widened.

Turning a corner, they saw that beds with patients lined the hallway.

"Say, where are you girls going?" A nurse wearing a starched white uniform suddenly stood behind them, hands on her hips.

"I'm looking for my brother," Grace said, trying to sound calm even though she was quaking with fear inside.

"Your brother?" The nurse smiled. "Well! You certainly won't find him in that direction! That's the Negro ward."

"Oh." Grace glanced at Joanna. "Well, we'll go the other way, then."

"No, I don't think so." The nurse was a large woman who seemed to tower over them.

Grace felt Joanna's grip get tighter.

"Tell me something," the nurse said. "Why would two nice girls like you want to be coming in here with all these bad germs? Don't you know tuberculosis is contagious?"

"We're not going to touch anyone!" Grace promised her. "And we'll only stay a couple minutes. *Please.* I need to see my brother. His name is Peter McFarland. Do you know my brother?"

"Do I know your brother?" The nurse repeated her question. "There are more than two hundred and twenty patients in here right now. Do I know Peter McFarland?" She pointed to the front door. "Back! The way you came."

Grace's shoulders slumped, but she obeyed.

"It's not just touching the patients, you understand," the nurse explained as she followed the girls. "Breathing the same air can be dangerous. I'll tell you what, though. We'll look up your brother in the directory and see how he's doing."

When they got to the lobby, Grace pulled the marbles from her pocket and turned around. "Maybe you could give him something for me."

The nurse stopped to look at the bag of marbles in Grace's outstretched hand. "I can't do that," she said. "We're not supposed to take things to the patients."

"But—"

The nurse walked past her and stepped behind a desk. After opening a large ledger, she ran a thick finger down over the names, muttering "McFarland, McFarland." She had to go on to another page before she stopped.

"Peter McFarland?" she asked, peering up at the girls.

"Yes," Grace confirmed.

The nurse removed her glasses. "Peter's very sick," she said. "Surely you know that."

Quickly, Grace opened the bag of marbles and fished inside for the blue agate, Pete's favorite shooter and his best hope for good luck. When she found it, she held it out.

"Please," she begged the nurse. "If Pete has his blue aggie, at least he'll have something to hold . . . while he's coughing."

The woman hesitated.

"Please?" Grace asked again.

And the nurse took the marble. "I'll see what I can do," she said.

Outside, it was raining again. The wind had picked up, too, and practically pushed the girls down the driveway. Grace let Joanna lead them back to the trolley line, where they stood, waiting for the next car to come.

Joanna made a fist and circled her heart, the sign for *sorry.*

Grace nodded. She would explain everything to Joanna later, she decided. On the trolley, however, Joanna slid her arm through Grace's and sat close beside her, and Grace knew that Joanna had understood.

Grace remained silent as they rode the trolley home. She should be used to disappointment by now, Grace thought as the car bounced and swayed. She knew only too well how cruel the world could be. Many times she had closed her eyes to sleep while her empty stomach turned with hunger. She had witnessed all of her family's possessions, like junk, tossed out onto the street. She had seen Pete's blood make a crimson blossom in the snow. And she worried she had destroyed Miss Louise's trust in her. . . .

So it did not come as a total surprise when, two days later, Uncle Stewart rang the doorbell at the Hammonds' house and stood, a stranger in the foyer, with his cap and driving gloves in his hands.

Grace knew before her foot hit the bottom stair why he was not smiling big and broad beneath his handlebar mustache.

Still, she thought, if she held back she could stop time and be spared. She did not know Uncle Stewart would reach out and take her hand so she couldn't get away.

"I'm so sorry," he said softly, changing her life forever, "but I have some sad news about Pete."

"Every Purpose Under the Heaven"

His marbles. Pete would want his marbles.

The next morning, while Uncle Stewart waited outside in the borrowed car, Grace ran back upstairs to grab the leather pouch from her cigar box and shoved it into her coat pocket.

In the front hallway, Miss Louise took Grace's hand and walked her out to Aunt Emma, who stood by the open car door, hunched from the cold. Aunt Emma gave Grace a long hug and then helped her into the backseat, where Grace sat quietly clutching a handkerchief and staring out the window.

As they headed out of the District, tall buildings, trolleys, and telephone poles blurred past. Grace rubbed at her tired, puffy eyes. It still seemed like a bad dream. How could Pete be gone? It was *not* fair. Grace never had a chance to say good-bye.

"Your mother and father are already out at the farm," Uncle Stewart explained. At Grampa Schmidt's farm there was a small family cemetery.

Aunt Emma, a black velvet hat on her head and a small veil covering her face, turned around and gave Grace the sign for *I love you.*

"Don't be sad, Grace." Uncle Stewart glanced quickly over his shoulder. "Pete is out of his misery now. He's with God."

Grace looked out the window again and tried to envision what it was like to be with God. Did it mean that Pete would never cough again? Would he stay the same age? In heaven, with God, would he have two arms the same?

After Uncle Stewart crossed the bridge over the Potomac River into Virginia, the scenery changed. No more buildings, just trees and fields, some with cows, one with a solitary donkey. At a tiny crossroads called Tysons Corners, Uncle Stewart stopped to get gas and asked Grace if she would like a Coca-Cola from the little store behind the gas pump.

"No thanks, I'm not thirsty," she said.

When he returned, Uncle Stewart handed her a chocolate bar. "Put it in your pocket for later," he told her.

Finally, Uncle Stewart announced they were in Arlington and soon afterward slowed down before turning up the long driveway to Grampa Schmidt's farm. A FOR SALE sign was nailed to a tree at the driveway's entrance.

Uncle Stewart stopped the car and sighed. "Times are difficult indeed," he said. "I don't know what's to become of us all."

Grace wondered where someone as old as Grampa Schmidt would go if he didn't have his farm.

It had been a long time since Grace last saw her grandfather. She didn't remember his hair being so white, or his face so full of wrinkles. He had always been an ornery dour man with a temper—a temper even quicker than Papa's. Grace and her brothers were afraid of him. Pete used to say Grampa

Schmidt was "as grouchy as a bear with a sore head." Even Mama and Papa walked as if on glass around him. That was probably why they so seldom visited.

On this day, however, Grampa Schmidt surprised Grace. With his gnarled, shaking hand he patted her lightly on the back (she couldn't remember ever hugging or kissing him) and motioned to where everyone had gathered.

It was a short walk to the cemetery, across an uneven field dotted with gray boulders. The ground lay hard, still partly frozen, beneath a dingy yellow blanket of grass pressed flat by the recent snow.

Up ahead, waiting, was a small group of people, including Papa, Mama holding Holly, and Uncle Fritz from Ohio. Grace recognized him right away despite a new dark beard. They stood inside a small fence that was missing boards and sorely in need of paint. It was too bad Pete had to be buried in such a run-down place, Grace thought. But then she spotted Grandma Rosa's thick white headstone and realized Pete would not be alone. A ring of tall, shaggy bark cedars guarded the cemetery, and high above the muffled small talk, Grace heard a mourning dove coo softly.

Uncle Fritz strode over to Grace and embraced her. His wiry whiskers brushed her face. Grace could see that he had the same kind eyes as Mama.

Suddenly, over Uncle Fritz's shoulder Grace saw that Pete's casket had already been lowered into the yawning, open ground. Grace felt her stomach lurch. When did they do that? she wondered. How would she get his marbles to him now? It was good that Owen and Iggy weren't here to see this.

She turned away, but she couldn't stop from crying.

Grampa Schmidt hobbled up beside her and put his hand on her back.

"I wanted to give Pete his marbles," Grace told him. She pulled them out of her pocket.

"I see," he said. He held up a long, bony finger. "I have an idea. If you leave them with me I'll make Pete a marker. I've got some cement mix. I'll make a block and put the marbles in it."

"You can do that?" Still sniffling, Grace looked up at this man who was both a stranger and a grandfather.

"I can. And I *will*," he assured her.

Grace took one marble from the bag, to keep forever, then handed the bag to her grandfather and went to stand beside Mama. Mama couldn't hold hands because of the baby, so Grace kept her hands pushed deep in her pockets. Even though she was surrounded by her own family, Grace had never felt more alone.

The Reverend Saunders began to read from the Bible. "To every thing there is a season, and a time to every purpose under the heaven." His voice rang clear in the frozen air. "A time to be born, and a time to die . . ."

The words upset Grace. Her mouth drew into a tight line. It was *not* Pete's time to die! What purpose did that serve? She wanted to scream. He had just turned fourteen, and it was going to be spring soon. Things were supposed to be beginning, not ending. Pete had so much to do! Pete was going to be president of the United States one day.

"A time to cast away stones, and a time to gather stones together . . ."

Her throat grew tight. *Gather together.* The phrase rang in her head. Together, she and Pete had secrets—secrets that would die with Pete. Grace knew she would never tell how she and Pete had sneaked after their father, as stealthy as the thieves they were, and watched him making corn liquor. No one would ever know that they spied through that little basement window by the coal chute. And no one would ever know that they got caught doing it.

The minister's mouth was moving, but Grace didn't hear the words. She was remembering how the man by the coal chute grabbed Pete by the front of his shirt and twisted it with his fist until it was right under Pete's chin. A deadly *click*—the man pressed a sharp blade against Pete's throat. It looked like the knife Papa used to take the guts out of fish. Grace screamed, and Pete—with that left-handed punch of his—came up right under that guy's arm and knocked the blade clear out of his hand into the lilac bush. *"Run, Grace, don't stop!"* Pete hollered as they dashed headlong through the dark streets toward home.

Mama was putting the little boys to bed when they got back. Breathless, Grace had crept into her room and took the Bible out from underneath the nightgowns in Mama's bureau drawer. With tears staining their cheeks, coal soot smeared on their hands, they had sworn they would never tell.

"A time to love, and a time to hate . . ."

Hate indeed. Grace *hated* the world that made her lose Pete, the best brother anyone could ever have. The night Mama had served rabbit stew, Pete got up and left. "A stomachache," he mumbled, because he knew.

"A time of war, and a time of peace."

When the minister had finished, Grace saw through bleary eyes that Mr. Ferguson from the old neighborhood was at the cemetery, lifting a fiddle to his shoulder. The opening note was long, and sad.

Papa reached over the hole to sprinkle dirt on Pete's coffin. And it was over.

Afterward, back in Washington, at the apartment with no windows, a few people gathered. Because there were only two chairs, most of them stood, drinking coffee and eating the apple pies that Mrs. Hammond had sent over. It didn't smell so bad in the room anymore. Mama had turned in the boxes with stinky dirt and received day-old bread in exchange. No mushrooms ever grew, she said. It was a waste of money.

"Where's Papa?" Grace asked.

Mama shrugged. "Gone for a walk, I guess. He's taking it hard. Do you think you could hold Holly for a while?"

With great care, Grace accepted the small bundle that was her sister. Then, slowly, she settled herself on the cold floor with her back against the wall and Holly in her arms.

Papa had probably stomped off in a huff, angry with Pete for dying. It wouldn't surprise Grace. He'd punch out God if he could.

With Holly resting on her arm, Grace could feel her sister's small back and the gentle rise and fall of her breathing. She watched how the baby yawned, oblivious to all the sadness around her. Holly would never know what a great brother she had. Someday, when Grace was older and they were both lying in the summer grass watching the clouds, Grace would tell her stories about Pete.

The Reverend Saunders set a plate beside her with apple pie and a fork. Grace stared at it, disinterested until she felt a gentle tug on her head. Holly had caught the end of one of Grace's braids with her tiny hand and was smiling and gurgling as she jerked the braid, unintentionally, back and forth. Grace grinned and noted how Holly had bright brown eyes like Pete's, and a miniature dimple in each dumpling of a cheek.

Mama touched the back of Grace's head. "We need to talk, you and me. Let's go outside."

Grace handed up the baby, and Mama passed her on to someone else.

Outside, it was gray and cold. Some boys were playing kick the can in the street. Grace finished buttoning her coat and stepped wide over a puddle made from melting snow.

Mama took her hand. "This way."

They walked on some, past the noisy boys to the corner where there was a run-down park with a broken swing set and one bench. The bench didn't have a back, but Mama said to "have a seat."

For a moment neither one of them said anything. It felt good to be out, in the quiet, away from everyone.

"We're all going to miss Pete," Mama said, her voice sounding more weary than it was sad. "I know how close you two were. I know how this hurts."

A lump rose in Grace's throat.

"I went to see him last week," Mama said.

"But I thought you couldn't visit there."

Mama shook her head. "You're not supposed to, no. But they knew Pete had a short time and I am his mother, after all."

Grace frowned as she stared at her hands. She wished she and Joanna could have found a way around that nurse.

"Did Pete know he was going to die?" Grace asked.

"Yes, I think so," Mama said. "But he was so sick by the end, Grace, that it probably came as a relief."

Tears gathered again in Grace's eyes, her mother's, too.

"Pete was glad you had written to him. He said, 'Tell Gracie to keep her good heart.'"

"Oh, Mama, I'm going to miss him so much," Grace cried, letting Mama hug her long and hard on that bench with no back. A good heart. That was easy. Grace could do that for Pete.

"There's more," Mama said, letting go so she and Grace could look at each other. "Papa and I—we've made a decision. I'm taking the boys and the baby and going home with Uncle Fritz to Ohio."

The world started to tip. Ohio? Where was that? Somewhere west of West Virginia? "Why?" Grace asked, astonished. "I thought Aunt Min had polio! And what about Papa?"

"I can't stay in that dreary basement another day, Grace. And it's precisely because of Aunt Min's polio that Uncle Fritz needs help running the house. There's a room off the kitchen where the kids and I can sleep. Papa's going to stay here and try to find work. He's stubborn. You know how he is. He says it'll be easier without us. A man alone can get shelter in the mission and go to the soup kitchen for a meal."

"What about me?" Grace asked.

"You can come with us, Grace." She paused. "Or you can stay with the Hammonds."

Grace waited.

"Miss Louise and I talked," Mama went on. "She and her husband are very fond of you. And she says you mean the world to Joanna. At the very least they want you to stay and finish the school year." Mama stopped again before saying it. "But they'd like to adopt you, Grace."

Miss Louise *did* still want her. Even after knowing she stole that pin.

"When did you talk to her?" Grace asked.

"Yesterday," Mama said.

Grace stared straight ahead, thinking.

"It might be best," her mother continued, in a voice that still didn't sound sad, or unsure, or regretful—just tired. It made Grace wonder if Mama was so worn out by life that she couldn't feel anymore.

"They can give you so much," Mama went on. "So much more than we can. You could always come visit us. I made sure of that."

Grace knew Mama was right. The Hammonds *could* provide—and Miss Louise needed her. Grace would only be a burden to her own family. And the rock-bottom truth was that not a particle of Grace wanted to go to Ohio and live in a room off Uncle Fritz's kitchen. Especially if Pete wasn't there. She would rather stay with the Hammonds, sleep in Miss Betsy's brass bed, and go to sixth grade at Oyster Grammar School. She could have said so right then, too, only she didn't want to hurt Mama's feelings.

Mama misunderstood her hesitation. "I know this is sudden," she said. "You don't have to decide right now. Certainly, you should finish school. But it wouldn't be fair to the Hammonds, you know, if you stayed on any longer.

"By summertime," Mama said, "you'll need to make up your mind."

Hope and Heartache

In the science room at school, Miss Fawcett placed a golden metal sun on the table. Attached to it in the back was a short handle. "I want you to turn the crank, Grace, and see what happens," she said.

But Grace already knew what would happen when you turned the crank. Rommy had told her. Tiny planets on thin metal wires would circle the sun. Some went faster than others, because each planet had a different orbit.

The crank was stiff and made a harsh, squeaking noise, but the planets moved. Everyone pressed close.

"Year in, year out, the planets orbit the sun." Miss Fawcett drew small circles in the air with her finger. "The planets' rotations create day and night."

Michael Lapinski raised his hand. "What I want to know, Miss Fawcett, is what happens if the sun explodes? Or dies out?"

Miss Fawcett's eyebrows arched. "Think of all the ways we depend on the sun. Who can name some?"

More hands shot up. Many answers: food; warmth; even clothes, because the fibers came from plants.

"So you see," Miss Fawcett said, "without the sun we would perish."

Grace stopped turning the crank. If they perished, then they would all be with God, she thought. She would see Pete again.

It was like this for several days. Every conversation, everything she saw or did, coming back to the fact that her brother was gone. Grace was caught off guard by how deeply his death had cut into her life.

"I'm so sorry," Miss Louise had said to Grace when she returned after the funeral. "I know how much you loved your brother."

They sat on the front steps that night. It was cold but clear, and the stars were out. Someone had told Grace once that heaven was up there, hidden from the world by an enormous swath of dark velvet, and that the stars were mere pinpricks in the curtain, allowing a little bit of heaven's light to shine through.

"There's a hole in my life now," Grace had replied. "Just like yours."

Miss Louise's eyes had filled with tears, but she reached out to put an arm around Grace's shoulders. "You just have to learn how to walk around it."

Joanna felt Grace's suffering, too. Every day, when Grace arrived home from school, there was a small surprise awaiting her. Something Joanna had made: a tiny watercolor of a tulip, a handmade bookmark, a poem about spring, a hair ribbon wrapped in tissue.

"You're a good friend," Grace told her.

"More than friend," Joanna wrote on a piece of paper. "We be sisters if you stay."

Not even Johnny could get Grace to laugh, although he didn't stop trying.

"Hey, kid," he said one day as he and Grace and Miss Louise took a stroll through the zoo. "You ever ride a mule?"

"A mule?" Grace looked at him funny. He certainly knew how to get her attention.

"Yeah. A mule. You know, one of those animals looks like a horse only it's got those two tall ears?" He made ears with his two index fingers.

Grace had to smile. "I know what a mule is."

"Well, I was just thinking," he said. "We're taking a trip this summer to see my big brother in San Francisco. On the way out to California maybe we could hop on the train over to the Grand Canyon and ride those mules down the Bright Angel Trail. A friend in my law class did it last year and said it was the best thing he's ever done."

"Johnny! You never mentioned a mule ride to me!" Miss Louise exclaimed. "You know I don't like heights."

"Well, heck then. Grace and I'll go down. Maybe Joanna, too. You can have tea at the hotel and warm up the bathwater for us."

Grace wrapped her arm tight around Miss Louise's. "Don't worry," she told her, "I won't leave you alone. But I bet they'd give you a really nice mule if you came."

Miss Louise chuckled. "Well, maybe," she conceded warily, "if we went together, I might not be afraid."

Grace grinned. "California," she repeated dreamily. "With Joanna?"

"If we can convince Mother and Father," Miss Louise replied.

Already, Grace was wondering how to make the sign for *mule*.

Just then a huge brown bear stood up in his outdoor pen to rub his back against a tree, and they stopped to watch.

The excitement of the trip was seeping in. Grace imagined herself on that train to California, gawking out the window at the Great Plains. At oceans of desert sand! At the Rocky Mountains!

Grace knew that California was part of the package. If she was adopted, she would make the trip, because she was their daughter. Just as they would travel as a family to New York City in the fall to visit Miss Betsy and see Radio City Music Hall—the biggest theater in the world!

Mama had said it would be for the best. . . .

A chilly wind whipped at the back of Grace's neck. She took her arm from Miss Louise's and reached behind to turn up her coat collar and pull down her hat. Her smile disappeared.

Johnny made a pout face and cocked his head. "Is there anything at all that we can do to cheer you up?"

Grace had to grin again because his expression was so silly.

"As a matter of fact, there is," she replied, surprising him. There was something Grace had been thinking about for quite some time now. She turned to Miss Louise. "I'd like to get my hair cut."

"But it's so beautiful," Miss Louise responded. "So long and lovely."

"I want it short. Like *yours*," Grace declared. "I want it—different."

"What would your mother say?" Miss Louise asked. "What if—"

"Mama doesn't care," Grace cut her off.

For a moment, no one spoke.

In their silence, the bear enjoyed a good, long scratch on the rough bark. When he rolled his head back and grunted with pleasure, all three of them laughed, and Miss Louise reached for Grace's hand. "I'll take you to the Powder Box at Woodies tomorrow," she said, "and we'll have it cut any way you like."

There was no turning back. Grace squeezed her eyes shut while the hairdresser snipped away. Not that she regretted the decision. She was still the same old Grace deep inside, Owen and Iggy's big sister, a person with a good heart. But she was different, too. And she needed to show the world that she wasn't the same old *impudent* girl she was six months ago. She was Grace McFarland, a girl with good manners and good grammar. A girl who had a best friend and nice clothes. A girl who went to the movies and painted with watercolors. A girl who rode in automobiles and one day soon would take piano lessons and play in a recital and sleep overnight on the train.

Why was the haircut so painful, then? Because it was the first one she'd ever had? Because in cutting off her hair, Grace knew she was cutting off something she shared with her mother? Because deep in her heart she thought this would make the final decision easier?

Grace bit her bottom lip so hard it bled. She winced when she touched it and saw the spot of blood on her hand.

Miss Louise rushed to give her a handkerchief. Grace pressed the cloth to her lip, then realized the haircut was over and stared at her old friend, scattered in pieces on the floor. She hadn't planned on it, but suddenly she was on her knees, scooping up handfuls of long brown hair. Miss Louise helped her braid it, and Grace took it home to put in her cigar box. Everyone made a fuss over how cute her new bob was, but Grace couldn't bring herself to look in a mirror for three days.

For a while, it seemed, nothing could lighten her mood. Not even the morning Grace and Miss Louise returned from the bakery to find the Scarlottis, suitcases packed, waiting out front for a taxi.

"We're going to Nevada," Esterbelle explained. "My father was hurt on the dam."

"Not badly. He's going to be okay," Mrs. Scarlotti hastened to add. "But it's time we were together."

Grace stood with a box of pastries in her hands, a little bag on top that held a large sugar cookie, her treat for polishing the silverware that morning.

The two girls looked at each other. Grace wanted to say she was sorry they had not been friends. Real friends who had fun and trusted each other. But she couldn't bring herself to say anything. And Esterbelle, who might have offered up an apology of her own, was equally silent.

"Here's our taxi!" Mrs. Scarlotti announced. "Come, Ester."

Esterbelle picked up her satchel and turned to go.

"Wait!" Grace snatched the little bag from atop the pastries and gave it to Esterbelle. "For the train," she said. "It's a big cookie with colored sugar."

Esterbelle took the bag, then flicked her eyes at Grace and walked away.

Pleased at her generosity, Miss Louise patted Grace on the shoulder and went on into the house.

But Grace stood, scowling, and crossed her arms. Esterbelle hadn't even said thank you.

"Esterbelle!" Grace called sharply. There were all kinds of things she could holler, such as *I'm sorry I don't have any milk to go with that!*

The girl turned.

Grace sucked in her breath. "Good luck!" she called out, holding up her hand in farewell.

And slowly, Esterbelle waved back.

The weather had changed its mind about any promise of spring. It was cloudy and cold that March day when the Scarlottis left and the new president arrived. Mr. and Mrs. Hammond, Miss Louise, Johnny, Grace, and Joanna bundled up and took the trolley downtown to the office where Miss Louise worked so they could watch the inaugural parade from inside.

"Jiminy, will you look at that?" Johnny said, pointing out the office window at the people who had gathered along Pennsylvania Avenue below. People of all ages not only packed the sidewalks and street, but crowded together to peer out of office-building windows everywhere. Still others braved the cold to stand on rooftops, while a few people climbed into the trees.

Presidents Hoover and Roosevelt rode by in a car, tipping their tall hats to the crowd, and a parade followed: marching bands, a wagonload of old soldiers from the Indian wars with long white whiskers, colorful floats. Grace and Joanna sat together looking out one window, drinking cups of hot chocolate from a thermos and watching wide-eyed the entire time.

"Oh, my!" Miss Louise pointed to a white-suited cowboy holding his hat high in the air while riding a prancing horse. "Isn't that Tom Mix?"

"Sure is," Johnny said. "There you go, girls, a real live film star!"

Fireworks were scheduled for that evening, too; but after they arrived home, Mrs. Hammond was shaking her head. "Enough is enough," she declared. Instead, they made popcorn and listened to President Roosevelt's inaugural address repeated on the radio. *"This great nation will endure as it has endured, will revive and will prosper. So, first of all, let me assert my firm belief that the only thing we have to fear is fear itself."*

"A grand speech," Miss Louise said.

Grace, who sat beside Miss Louise knitting her baby blanket for Holly, looked up and smiled. She knew that wherever Papa was, he was happy because Franklin Roosevelt was finally president.

"That man has given everyone hope," Johnny agreed. "Maybe he'll be the one to finally save this country."

Even Mama sounded optimistic in her first letter.

Dear Grace,

Uncle Fritz has made us feel right at home. Our room off the kitchen is tiny, but it's cozy. We have beds. We're warm at night—and no one is hungry. In the morning, while Uncle Fritz milks the cows, I cook a big breakfast with eggs, toast, and fresh milk. Aunt Min's little boy, Andy, is a sweetheart and loves having Iggy and Owen to play with. You should have seen them yesterday when one of the sheep gave birth. I think their eyes were about to pop out of their heads with amazement. Uncle Fritz has written a letter to the president, telling him what happened to us, how our family has had to split up. I told him don't be silly, but he says that President Roosevelt really cares and would want to know. . . .

Uncle Fritz wasn't the only person writing to the new president. Hundreds—*thousands*—of people wrote of their hope and heartache in the days following his inauguration. So many people—so many letters—that the president's staff needed to call on employees in other government offices to help in handling the mail.

"You won't believe this," Miss Louise said at dinner. "All of us girls were called into the boss's office today. He said if anyone wanted to assist with mail at the White House, we should report there tomorrow."

"Goodness, Louise, will you go?" Mrs. Hammond asked.

"Of course she will!" Mr. Hammond thundered from the end of the table.

Miss Louise looked down shyly. "Well, I don't know," she said softly. "It sounds exciting, but I've never worked outside of the Internal Revenue office. And it might mean longer hours. Saturdays, too, for while."

"But it's an opportunity!" Mr. Parker insisted, a fork full of green beans paused in midair. "You can't pass up an opportunity like that, Louise! Tell her, Johnny!"

Johnny grinned and shrugged. "She knows. It's up to her. Whatever she wants to do is fine with me."

Miss Louise turned to Grace. "What do you think, Grace?"

Grace's eyes widened. She felt very important to be asked her opinion. "I think you should do it," she said. "It'll be fun!"

"But I won't know anyone—" Miss Louise began.

"I didn't know anyone when I came here," Grace reminded her. "And look at me!"

Indeed, Grace thought, *look at her.* Look at what had become of poor Grace McFarland since the snowy night she came to the Hammonds' house.

"Besides," Grace added soberly, "President Roosevelt needs your help."

Miss Louise smiled at her, then glanced back at all the faces around the table. "Then it's decided," she declared. "I shall go work at the White House tomorrow."

A cheer rose from the table. And each day thereafter Miss Louise captivated the diners with tidbits from her new assignment. "I saw President Roosevelt today. He was in the hallway, being pushed in his wheelchair. . . . Mrs. Roosevelt came through the office with her Scottish terrier. . . . They've offered me a permanent job there! Yes! Working as a secretary to Stephen Early in the press office. . . . Sit down, all of you. Today I took dictation from the president himself!"

Mrs. Hammond, both hands on her face, could barely contain herself. "Oh, my dear, Louise, weren't you too excited to take shorthand?"

"I was a nervous Nellie!" she admitted. "But the president put me right at ease. He was getting his hair cut when I entered with my steno pad. 'Hell-o. I appreciate your coming over to do this. I'd like you to take a letter to the editor of *The New York Times*,' he said to me."

Grace's own favorite story, however, was of the man who showed up at the White House with a trained duck and requested an audience with the president. "It's unbelievable!" Miss Louise kept saying. "Any Tom, Dick, or Harry can walk in off the street and ask to see the president. Of course, it doesn't mean they get in. I had that duck walking around my desk all afternoon!"

For weeks, no one mentioned the decision Grace still had to make.

Grace already felt as though she was part of the Hammond family. She knew she had slipped comfortably into a new life. There were nine dresses in the closet now. Piano lessons had started. And every other day, Grace took a bath in the claw-foot tub down the hall, drying herself off afterward with a thick, clean towel.

Only the occasional letter from Mama stirred up unsettled

feelings: *Iggy and Owen hate the outhouse, but Uncle Fritz is talking about getting indoor plumbing by next year—if the price of milk doesn't go down anymore. . . . Holly is sitting up now. . . . Oh, and the lambs, Grace. They're so sweet. . . .*

Then, one day, Miss Louise took Joanna and Grace to the annual Easter Egg Roll at the White House. . . .

Under a bright sun they tromped with hundreds of others across the south lawn of the White House. A radio broadcast reported forty-seven thousand people had turned out for the egg roll. Indeed, it seemed to Grace like a rolling sea of heads and hats. What everyone had come for was not a chance to roll an egg or hear the marine band play, however, but to get a glimpse of the new president.

He rewarded them finally, waving briefly from the South Portico. Grace and Joanna stood on their tiptoes to see.

"And do you see that little girl up there? The one with the pink frock and the chestnut hair?" Miss Louise asked the girls. "That's the Roosevelts' granddaughter, Sistie. She's six. And that little boy with the white beret? It's their grandson, Buzzie."

It happened on the way home. Traffic was thick and the trolley moved slowly. Grace's new black Easter shoes had worn a blister on the back of her heel. She leaned forward to unbuckle the strap and rub the sore spot when she noticed out the window a long line of ragged men in overcoats, most of them smoking.

Grace sat up. "Who are they?" she asked Miss Louise.

Joanna pointed out the window, and Miss Louise leaned over to see.

"Men out of work probably. There's a soup kitchen at that

church. Do you see that table there? They'll get a bowl of soup and a piece of bread."

Grace tucked her hair behind her ear and stared sadly at the row of grim, unshaven faces. She was afraid she would see Papa—and she did. She couldn't see his face; he was staring at the ground, his hands in his pockets. But Grace was sure it was him. She recognized the tweed cap he wore.

Poor Papa, she thought. He looked so thin and haggard. Could this really be the same man who had played the fiddle with such vigor? Who railed at the men threatening to evict them? Who lovingly transformed empty Spam cans into a Christmas train?

The trolley didn't move. Grace's eyes remained glued to her father. He shuffled forward a step, his chin lifting slightly, and a memory from long ago skirted Grace's mind: the day Papa saved her from drowning in the river when she slipped in off the bank. She was only three or four, but she still remembered the cold shock of muddy brown water, the dirt taste of it, and how the world went dark. Papa had pulled her out with one strong motion, then wrapped her in his big flannel shirt and carried her all the way home.

Grace blinked as tears clouded her vision. Although it was warm outside, she suddenly felt very cold, especially her hands, which lay clenched in her lap. A soup line meant that Papa still had not found a job. Grace wished she could do something to help him. But what?

Her heart pounded as she moved one hand up to tap on the window. Then, at the last moment, she pulled it back. Papa would feel ashamed if he knew Grace had seen him standing in a soup line, like a beggar. Slowly, she shrank away from the window.

What if Papa never found work? What if Mama, Iggy, Owen, and Holly had to stay in Ohio with Uncle Fritz forever?

Ohio seemed so far away. But at least they were together, Grace thought. With fresh milk for breakfast and cute lambs in the barn . . .

Grace covered her mouth with her hand. She could never give up what she had now. . . . *Never!*

"Do you know what you want, Grace?" Miss Louise asked.

Startled, Grace dropped her hand and turned.

Miss Louise smiled sweetly. "When we get to Jolson's Pharmacy. Do you know what flavor ice cream you want?"

SPRING

Finally, spring stepped forth beneath a bright blue canopy of sky and the world outside shed its dull winter colors. Purple and white crocuses popped up in greening patches of lawn, and bright yellow daffodils fringed the sidewalks.

Mornings were still cool, but Grace found that the sweater she wore buttoned up when she walked to school came home in the afternoon tied around her waist as she skipped up the sidewalk.

There was a feeling of excitement in the air. Squirrels chased one another up the tree trunks, and at the zoo the baby elephant ran playful circles around his mother.

During recess, the girls teased one another during games of double Dutch on the hardtop.

Down in the meadow
where the green grass grows,
there sat Grace
as sweet as a rose.
She sang, she sang,

she sang so sweet.
Along came Rommy,
who kissed her on the cheek.
How many kisses
did she get?
One, two, three, four, five . . .

Grace's cheeks grew warm every time she replayed it in her mind. She wondered if Rommy had heard it while he was swinging his bat, or if someone had told him later.

At school, Grace—and all her friends who had been to see *The Three Little Pigs* at the movie theater—were singing "Who's afraid of the Big Bad Wolf?" And in the Hammond household there was talk of the California trip, of fishing off the pier at Chesapeake Beach in Maryland, and of going to the circus, which set up every year near Union Market.

"You need see this man Clyde Beatty! Incredible!" Joanna told Grace in a rushed combination of finger spelling and sign. "Chain in his left hand, whip in right hand. Pistol on thigh. Forty tigers and lions! Amazing!"

Grace chuckled, not just in anticipation, but because she loved the sign for *amazing*. Both hands near the eyes, thumb and index finger pressed together, then opening quickly to indicate an eye-popping sight.

Miss Louise worked long hours at the White House, but she was exhilarated by her new surroundings and the famous people she saw each day.

"Mrs. Roosevelt had all the secretaries to a luncheon in the Rose Garden today," she recounted one evening at dinner.

"When she passed me the pickles, I almost dropped the dish!"

Everyone laughed.

"But you know," Miss Louise continued, "when we finished eating, Mrs. Roosevelt took out her knitting, and we sat there chatting. All of us. Just like old friends."

In the evenings Miss Louise, Grace, and Joanna took out their own knitting. Or sometimes Miss Louise helped Grace with her piano lesson, or they worked together, clipping articles from a stack of accumulated newspapers for Miss Louise's White House scrapbook.

"Someday, when you don't have school, I'll take you into the office with me," Miss Louise promised as they cut and pasted. "Who knows? Maybe you'll get to meet the president!"

"Oh, Miss Louise. That would be so exciting," Grace exclaimed. "What would I wear? Oh—and do you think I could ask about a job for Papa?"

Miss Louise paused. "I'm sure you could ask him just about anything, Grace. President Roosevelt would listen."

Papa needed work. He couldn't stay at the mission and eat at the soup kitchen forever. Grace had thought of asking Miss Louise to take her to see him there—or to invite him over for dinner, but then she worried that Papa would be ashamed. She decided to wait; she knew he would come to see her when the time was right.

It made Grace sad to think of her father, especially when there were so many good things happening in her life. In June she would turn twelve. Miss Louise had asked her what she wanted and Grace had told her, "A pair of roller skates and a chocolate cake with candles." Soon after that school would be over. Already Miss Fawcett had announced that everyone in the class would be promoted to the seventh grade. There was no question that Grace wanted to be with them in the fall. She would have stories about sleeping on the train and riding a mule into the Grand Canyon.

But then a letter would come from Mama. . . .

Dear Grace,

Holly can crawl. She loves Uncle Fritz's cat, Sam, and crawls around the house following Sam all day. I swear her first word is going to be meow. *Oh, and she's standing up, holding onto things, of course. Pretty soon I think she'll be walking. . . . Aunt Min had an old brown wicker perambulator, and the boys have enjoyed pushing Holly around in it. . . .*

Did you know that Grampa Schmidt has moved out here, too? We made a room for him in the attic and, wonder of wonders, he is a blessing to us all. He was heartbroken over losing his farm. But it's changed him. He's more patient now. He enjoys the children and is glad to be of some use. Yesterday, he helped a cow deliver a calf that was stuck. Incredible.

Papa still doesn't have a job. I told him to come out with us. Uncle Fritz could use his help, too. And at least he'd be eating well and have a decent place to sleep. But you know Papa; he's too proud. He says he's an electrician, not a farmer. . . .

Owen and Iggy gather the eggs for Uncle Fritz. . . . Aunt Min named the new calf Eleanor in honor of the First Lady . . . and you should see this billy goat. He's so ornery, he butts at everything—even the tree stump in his pen. He reminds me of the way Grampa Schmidt used to be. There is a new litter of kittens in the barn. . . .

Grace's eyes fell away from the words on paper. She wondered what it would be like to push her baby sister in the brown wicker perambulator. She longed for a good look at that billy goat. And her arms ached to hold a kitten.

Miss Louise had assured Grace that she could visit Mama anytime she wanted. Grace touched the back of her neck and felt the strange, blunt edge of her short new bob, and something twisted deep inside. Seeing her family would never be the same, would it? Grace would be a visitor, with a suitcase and a return ticket. And Pete wouldn't be there. . . .

So it hung over Grace's head, this decision she still had to make. It lingered overhead like a solitary cloud that suddenly appears from out of nowhere, throwing a shadow onto the sunniest of days and creating a dark and wobbly thing in her chest.

"Grace, I'd like you to read the Bible verse for us this morning."

Class had just finished the Pledge of Allegiance. Grace took her hand from her heart and walked up to the front of the room, where Miss Fawcett opened the Bible and indicated with her finger where she should start and stop.

It was a long verse from Ecclesiastes. Grace recognized it right off as the one the Reverend Saunders had read at Pete's funeral. Of all the verses in the Bible, she thought, why this one? Grace took a deep breath and glanced quickly at Miss Fawcett, because even if her teacher didn't know what a painful reminder this verse was to Grace, it still didn't seem fair to have to read such a long one when everyone else got something shorter, from Psalms or Proverbs.

"Go ahead, Grace," Miss Fawcett encouraged her.

Grace swallowed hard. "To every thing there is a season," she began, a bit shakily, "and a time to every purpose under the heaven. A time to be born, and a time to die . . ." Line by line, her voice grew stronger. "A time to weep, and a time to laugh; a time to mourn, and a time to dance . . ."

When she finished, she handed the heavy Bible back to Miss Fawcett and sat down at her desk.

Miss Fawcett wanted to talk about it.

"A time to cast away stones, and a time to gather stones together. Now I like that one," she declared. "Because our country is going through difficult times. Getting people to work together is what the president is trying to do."

Grace wondered on the walk home if there was also a time for knowing when, and how, to make the right decision.

At home in the Hammonds' house that afternoon, Grace was greeted by the comforting smell of salt-rising bread—as well as by another letter, which had been left propped up on the small table in the front hall next to the telephone.

After setting down her book bag, Grace picked up the letter. She admired the purple three-cent stamp with George Washington's face, and the way Mama had written *Miss Grace McFarland* in neat cursive.

Just as she began to tear open the envelope, Mrs. Hammond came down the stairs with a finger in front of her lips. "Shhhhh, Joanna's asleep."

"Is her cold worse?" Grace whispered.

Mrs. Hammond motioned for Grace to follow her into the kitchen. "Much worse," she said gravely when they got inside the swinging door. "She's started wheezing, poor thing." She cut a slice of warm bread for Grace. "Let me get you a glass of milk, too."

Grace wished Joanna didn't get sick so often because then they couldn't be together. "Is there anything I can do?" she asked.

"No, dear." Mrs. Hammond shook her head. "I don't think so."

Grace could tell by the way she sighed that she was worried.

When Mrs. Hammond went back upstairs, Grace drank the milk and took her bread outside to eat on the front porch glider while she read the letter from Mama.

Dear Grace,

I'm so glad to hear that Joanna has become such a dear friend. It made me realize how much I miss Aunt Emma. We talked about everything. It's not the same writing every few weeks. . . . Oh, and we all loved hearing about that new dance—the "chicken scratch"—that Johnny taught you and Joanna. I never heard of it—or the "kangaroo dip"! You'll have to teach us when you come. . . .

What did Mama mean—"when you come"? Did she mean when Grace went out to visit? Grace smiled, imagining the gig- gling that would go on when she taught Iggy and Owen how to "chicken scratch" by putting their hands on their hips, flapping their elbows, and sticking out their chests.

> *It's only June and already it's hot. We sit on the porch evenings. Uncle Fritz lights a few cow pies to keep the mosquitoes away and then lifts the battery out of the truck and hooks it up to the radio on the porch so we can listen to the ball game out of Chicago. We're all Cubs fans now. . . .*

Grace frowned. How could they listen to baseball and not think of Pete? Her eyes grew misty. The Washington Senators were off to a great start this season, but every time someone even mentioned baseball Grace blocked it out.

> *There's no word from Papa. He's not a writer. But there was a note from Aunt Emma. She said Uncle Stewart had driven Papa out to Pete's grave a couple times. . . .*

Papa? Sitting beside Pete's grave? Grace lowered her hands, and the letter, down to her lap and gazed off to the side, where a soft breeze stirred the yellow forsythia bush outside the porch. Despite Papa's temper, his impatience, Pete had always looked up to him. Grace remembered how Pete's eyes shone with admiration whenever Papa picked up his fiddle to play. With his one good hand, Pete would slap his knee and tap his foot. And Grace never saw Pete smile so broadly as when he and Papa were jumping out of their seats together to cheer a home run at Griffith Stadium.

Grace tried to finish the letter—

How's the knitting coming along? Are you still working on that blanket for Holly?

—but suddenly, Mrs. Hammond's panicked voice on the telephone just inside the front door broke the quiet afternoon.

"Dr. Posner's office? This is Mrs. Hammond. . . . My daughter Joanna, yes. I talked to you earlier. I'm very concerned. She's having trouble breathing. Can he come quickly? Please!"

"A Time to Gather Stones Together"

Grace hung back in the doorway and winced when she heard the deep, wet rumble in Joanna's chest.

"Please, Grace!" Mrs. Hammond turned with a worried look. "Run into the basement and get Mr. Hammond. He's fixing the furnace. Hurry!"

Grace sprinted from the room and dashed down the stairs.

"You need to come!" she exclaimed when she found Mr. Hammond sitting on a stool with a wrench in his hands. "Joanna's having trouble breathing!"

Mr. Hammond set down the tool and rushed back to Joanna's room with Grace.

"The doctor's on his way," Mrs. Hammond said.

Joanna's father took her hand. "You'll be all right," he promised.

"Grace, could you please wait by the front door and show Dr. Posner up when he arrives?" Mrs. Hammond asked.

Joanna rolled her head on the pillow and lifted a weak hand to wave.

"Be strong," Grace said, making the sign for *strong* with two fists at the chest and moving them forward. It came automatically, and she did it without thinking, or caring, that Mr. Hammond was sitting right there watching as she signed. No one cared. Not then.

In the front yard, Grace paced. She picked up a stick and broke it. She worried that if Pete could die, then maybe Joanna could, too. "No!" she said out loud, kicking a small stone into the hedge. Joanna was her best friend. Joanna was practically her sister. It couldn't happen to Grace twice!

The doctor finally arrived, with Miss Louise right behind him. She and Grace waited in the upstairs hallway while Joanna was examined. When Dr. Posner was through, he repacked his small leather bag, and everyone followed him downstairs.

"It's developed into pneumonia," he told them in the living room.

Mrs. Hammond put a hand over her mouth.

"You've been through this before with Joanna. Keep her warm and comfortable. Try to get the fever down.

"She's weak," Dr. Posner continued. "Keep her sipping on something. Beyond that, there's nothing more we can do. I'll be back in the morning to check."

Late in the evening, Miss Betsy arrived in a taxi from the train station, but there was no fanfare, no "welcome home" cake or souvenirs from New York City. People moved quietly through the house and talked in whispers. Even Mr. Parker stopped typing.

Grace set the table in the dining room for the boarders and helped Miss Betsy fix trays with soup, bread, and pudding. But she herself didn't eat until the Hammonds made sandwiches later. Afterward Grace washed all the dishes and wiped off the counters. She set out coffee cups for the morning and swept the floor.

When she was finished, she joined Mr. Parker, who was reading in the front room. But all she could think about was Joanna's feverish face, her weak hand. Grace put aside her own book to knit—and ended up finishing Holly's blanket. It was way past her bedtime. A somber mood filled the house. At eleven o'clock Johnny stopped playing solitaire at the dining-room table, ran his hand through his hair, and said to Grace, "You ought to get some sleep."

Because Miss Betsy was home, Grace put herself to bed in the rollaway, pulling the red afghan up to her chin and closing her hands tightly with prayers for Joanna.

The days that followed dragged by with little change. Grace put her book bag in her room after school and sat outside Joanna's closed door with her knees drawn up and her back against the wall. Even the last day of school passed without much notice.

"You must prepare yourselves for the worst," Dr. Posner told them.

The fever had spiked again. Joanna struggled to breathe.

Prepare yourself. Grace could not figure out how you did that; how you prepared yourself for the worst. Put on a suit of armor? Lock yourself in a room? Run away? What could you possibly *do* to ward off bad news? She remembered walking down the stairs to Uncle Stewart. If she had barricaded herself in her room, would it have stopped Pete from dying?

Miss Louise stayed home from work, and she and Miss Betsy took turns with their parents sitting with Joanna so that she was never alone. The comforting sounds of their voices came under the door with the soft light from Joanna's room. Grace wondered as she listened: Were they signing as they spoke? Writing notes?

"Joanna, do you remember back in West Virginia, that time when we thought you were lost?" It was Miss Louise's voice. "We called and called, but of course, you couldn't hear. You were in the shed with Scarlet and her puppies. How you loved that dog."

"We had half the town out looking for you," Miss Betsy added.

There was a pause. Joanna must have signed something.

"You miss Scarlet? Gentle, yes. She was the sweetest dog we ever had."

When Mr. Hammond visited, he sounded desperate and made repeated promises, as though he could somehow *bribe* Joanna into getting better. "When you're well, Joanna, we'll take a trip to Maine. Grace has never eaten lobster. . . . When you feel better, we'll pack a picnic supper and go to Haines Point. You know how much you love watching the boats go by. . . ."

One day when he left the room, Grace met him in the hall. "Mr. Hammond," she said, "if you really want Joanna to look forward to something, why don't you promise her that she can go to a school for the deaf? It's what she wants more than anything else in the world."

Mr. Hammond stared at her but said nothing. Grace felt her hands curl tightly at her sides. She knew she'd been brazen— maybe even impudent. But she didn't care if she had offended him. If Joanna died, nothing would matter anyway.

Suddenly, she heard Miss Louise and Miss Betsy talking to Joanna again. There were gaps in between the conversation. Grace sat on the floor and leaned her back against the wall. She heard the splashing of a rag being wrung out in a bowl of cool water, the scrape of a chair pulled up beside the bed.

"Are you cold, Joanna?" Miss Louise said these words out loud, although she may have been signing, too.

"Do you want to sleep?" Miss Betsy asked.

"Of course. We know we don't have to stay," Miss Louise was saying. "We *want* to, Joanna."

"I remember the time I had the measles." Miss Betsy's voice this time. "You must have been five years old, Joanna. You would come in, like this, and sit at my bedside. Put a cloth on my head, like Mother."

Memory after memory, like loose threads woven into a tap-estry that told a family's story. As Grace listened, she heard how they had pulled together through difficult times. She recalled how Mr. Hammond had sold his store in West Virginia and how they all had moved here, to Washington, to "start a new life."

She began to think of all the places her own family had moved in the last two years. The memories flashed like a news-reel through Grace's mind: hauling water at six in the morning, stuffing cardboard in her boots, finding the furniture piled on the street. She thought of Pete, coughing; of Papa, standing in line for free soup because there was no work and then sitting by Pete's lonely grave out in that field in Virginia.

It would be so easy, she thought, to put it all behind her. To simply stay with the Hammonds—with Joanna for a sister, if God let her live. *Please, God, let her live.* Mama said she wanted Grace to have a good life. And it's not as though she would never see her family again.

But Grace squirmed uncomfortably with these thoughts. Because she knew if she stayed she would always wonder what it would have been like to grow up with Iggy and Owen, and Holly, her little sister. Good times were bound to come again for her family—just as they had for the Hammonds.

She held her head in her hands because it hurt. It hurt to realize that if a family really wanted to stay together, it had to hold tight, good times *and* bad. What was it the Reverend Saunders had said? It had to gather those stones together.

A Ticket, a Trunk, a Train

"Some toast, please." Joanna spelled out her simple request slowly, on her fingers.

"Did you see that? Did you *hear* that?" Mrs. Hammond came into the upstairs hall, and her joyous voice rang out. "Joanna wants toast!"

There were only two people home at the time—Grace and Miss Louise—but they came running from the kitchen.

Joanna was still weak and plagued by a lingering cough. But she had turned the corner on her illness. The fever was gone and her appetite was returning. She was smiling. She was going to pull through!

Grace was allowed back in to visit, and for hours at a time she stayed at Joanna's side, signing, talking, writing notes, playing cards. Together, the girls planned their future. "We'll be teachers," they had agreed, Grace giving Miss Louise the news one day. "Teachers for the deaf," Grace pointed out. "I'm going to keep working on my sign language until I'm just as good as Joanna!"

"Shhh!" Miss Louise looked back at the doorway. "You don't want Father to hear you talking like that—"

"Don't you know?" Grace cut her off. "He said Joanna can go to school! A school for the deaf! He promised her if she got better!"

Joanna made the sign for *learn* and pointed to herself as she nodded with a broad smile of victory.

"When did *that* happen?" Miss Louise sat on the bed and opened her arms to embrace them both. Grace reached around to return the hug and closed her eyes. They didn't know yet. Grace had not told them of her decision.

The next evening, as Miss Louise sat at the dining-room table, scissors in hand, surrounded by piles of newspaper clippings and a pot of glue, Grace came in to watch—and wait for the right moment.

"Working on your scrapbook?"

Miss Louise grinned at her. "Ummmm. If I don't keep up with it, it'll be too overwhelming."

From the pile Grace picked up a small pencil drawing of a dog. "He's so cute."

"That's Mrs. Roosevelt's Scottie dog, Meggie. A guy named Charlie Thompson did that."

"Why are you keeping this?" Grace asked, squinting at a Peoples Drugstore ad for "All you can drink of our Buttermilk 5 cents."

Miss Louise took it and flipped it over. "Here. The other side is an article on the Easter Egg Roll. We won't forget that, will we? Look at the headline: 'Forty-five Children Lost on Day of Festivities.'"

"Whoa—I didn't know *that* happened!" Grace pulled out a chair and sat, while Miss Louise clipped with her scissors, browsing through other articles. On the back of one newspaper story was part of a train schedule for the B & O Railroad: $3.00 for a ticket to Philadelphia, $1.25 to Baltimore, and $12.00 to Cincinnati.

Cincinnati was in Ohio. Uncle Fritz's farm was in Ohio.

Grace looked up and watched Miss Louise trim the edges from a photograph of Mrs. Roosevelt.

"I've decided," Grace said.

Miss Louise stopped cutting.

Their eyes met.

Grace swallowed hard. She nodded. "I've decided," she repeated. "I need to go home to my family."

Miss Louise slowly rested her hands on the table. "Are you sure?" she asked in a strange voice as soft as a whisper.

Tears were pooling in Grace's eyes. She moistened her lips. "Yes. It was *you*, Miss Louise—you and Miss Betsy, who helped me decide. Listening to the way you talked to Joanna, I realized I needed to grow up with my own sister, and my brothers, too. Just like your family—just like the Hammonds had hard times— well, so did the McFarlands. Maybe someday things will be better for us—like they are for you—and we'll be together."

Grace paused, hoping she was explaining it right, and could see the tears gathering in Miss Louise's eyes, too.

"I know you need me," Grace said.

When Miss Louise nodded, Grace clapped a hand over her mouth and was seized with the terrible feeling that she had made the wrong decision.

Miss Louise reached over for her hands, and Grace grabbed them.

"But my mama needs me, too," Grace finished in a rush.

"I *do* understand, Grace," Miss Louise told her. "I do."

Letting go of Grace's hands, Miss Louise stood. Then Grace pushed back her chair and rushed to hug her, and they both cried together.

It was hardest with Joanna. Hardest because even before Grace said anything, Joanna knew, and her eyes filled with tears.

"You, Joanna," Grace said, pointing, "you and your sisters showed me how important it was for a family to stay together."

"I understand," Joanna assured her in sign, "but it hurts."

There was a trip to Uncle Stewart's and Aunt Emma's to say good-bye. And a visit to the cemetery at what had been Grampa Schmidt's farm in Arlington so that Grace could kneel in the grass and touch the smooth ring of marbles in the rough cement block over Pete's grave. Her grandfather had fulfilled his promise to put up a real marker. A small one, rising a full foot above the ground, was inscribed PETER ALOYSIUS McFARLAND. AT PEACE. 1919–1933.

When it was time to pack, Grace discovered that she had far too many things to fit into a single satchel. Mr. Hammond climbed into the attic and found her a big black trunk with a brass lock and thick leather handles. Carefully, the dresses and sweaters were folded and placed inside. Even the green dress from the mission was packed.

Underneath the clothing, Grace settled the cigar box that

contained her braid, the little bird from Grandma Rosa's cuckoo clock, Pete's letter, and the infamous list. Maybe one day, she thought, she could still make good on that list. At the very least, she could repay Mr. Hewitt for the gold pocket watch she and Pete had taken. On top of the clothes, Grace placed the pink blanket for Holly.

Other things were squeezed into spaces between clothes: the letters from Mama, the books Joanna had given her, the new roller skates, Grace's doll. Already Grace was thinking she might give her doll to Holly, when Holly was a little older.

On her twelfth birthday, Miss Louise had given Grace a small pocketbook so she could carry a few things—a comb, a handkerchief, some mints, a few coins for soda pop—as well as the train ticket to Cincinnati.

"We will write to each other," Miss Louise said for the second time as she hugged Grace outside her waiting train. Miss Louise was struggling with all the good-byes. Grace knew her heart had been broken.

"I didn't know I had it in me to love another child, ever again," Miss Louise told her, squeezing so hard Grace had to hold her breath. "But you showed me I could." She released Grace and held her at arm's length. "You can come back to visit, you know. Anytime you want."

Joanna nodded in agreement. Her cough was almost gone, but she was bundled up heavily for the trip to Union Station, and a large kerchief framed her small, sweet face. She hooked her index fingers together for *friends* and signed to Grace that it would *be forever.*

Grace swallowed hard. "Tell me all about school," she said, trying hard not to cry and hoping Joanna understood without Grace finger spelling. "I will write to you about the farm."

Then Grace put her right hand over the left, which rested on her heart, the sign for *love*.

Joanna's eyes glistened. The girls hugged.

"All aboard!" the conductor hollered.

A loud bell clanged. People in the waiting crowd finished their good-byes. Grace's heart beat fast.

"We'll keep trying to find your father," Miss Louise said hurriedly, releasing Grace from a final embrace. "Don't worry. We left word at the mission where he was staying. He knows you're leaving today."

It disappointed but did not surprise Grace that Papa had not made it down to the station to see her off.

"Hurry," Mrs. Hammond urged. "You'll want a seat by the window."

"Thank you. Thank you, all of you," Grace said. Miss Louise hugged her one last time.

The trunk was already on board. A uniformed porter was reaching out a hand to help Grace up the steps.

Seated on the train and looking through the filmy window at the Hammond women outside, Grace kept waving to stop from trembling inside. She told herself that Miss Louise would be all right. Her new job kept her busy. Maybe she didn't even know it yet, but that hole in her life was getting filled in with work. Miss Louise had promised she would look up Sarah at the mission. But even if Sarah was gone, there would be another little girl, or boy. Maybe one day Miss Louise would even have children of her own. Grace knew this was possible, because she was a firm believer in guardian angels. Two of them had saved her once.

And Joanna would make lots of friends at her new school. A whole new world awaited her.

There was a jolt. The train moved slightly. Grace clutched the little pocketbook in her lap. Beside her was a box stuffed with sandwiches, apples, and slices of chocolate cake from her birthday party.

Slowly, the train moved forward. Grace turned around to wave out the window one last time and felt warm tears spill onto her cheeks.

Then, suddenly, a breathless voice from behind startled her. "Excuse me, is this seat taken?"

Grace looked up to see her father standing with a battered suitcase in one hand, his fiddle case in the other.

"Almost didn't make it!" he said as if he'd been expected.

"Papa!" Grace exclaimed.

He set the fiddle case down and pointed to the seat. "Do you mind if I go along?"

Disbelieving, Grace shook her head slowly and began to smile. She knew he would come when the time was right!

Papa hoisted his two cases up to a luggage rack above the seat and then sat down heavily beside Grace. "Nothing for me here anymore," he said, letting his opened hands drop on his legs. "When I got the note that you were leaving, I thought to myself, The whole family is out there now. We may as well go together—you and me, Grace—to see what the McFarlands can find in Ohio."

Grace felt her eyes widen even more, her mouth drop. "Does Mama know you're coming?"

"Nope." Papa grinned, breaking all the hard lines in his face; and as the train picked up speed, it struck Grace that she hadn't seen the corners of her father's mouth turn upward in a very long time.

"It'll be a surprise," he said, his eyebrows lifting at his own understatement.

Papa hugged her and Grace hugged him back, pushing her face into the rough wool of a worn coat she'd never seen before. It smelled of smoke and wear and unknown places, but inside it was her father, and that was all that mattered.

"Grampa Schmidt is kind of frail, I hear," Papa told Grace as he released her. "And Uncle Fritz said he could use another strong hand with those cows. You reckon I could learn?"

Grace nodded vigorously and grinned. "Yes! Me, too! I can help with the cows and everything!"

"Say, I like that fancy new hairdo," Papa said.

Grace touched her short hair, the bangs that brushed her eyebrows. "It'll grow long again," she said. "It's already grown practically an inch!"

There was a pause. Papa was thinking about something else.

"I hear tell that farm's got a pond loaded with bass," he said. "Think Owen and Ig are old enough to do some fishin' with us?"

"Sure I do. They're ready to learn, Papa." Grace said this with exuberance, but there was nevertheless a tug at her heart, because she remembered that it was Pete who had always baited her hook. Grace hated the feel of those slimy worms. But she would have to do it now. She might even have to do it for Iggy and Owen, too. A ring of marbles came into her mind. Grace reached into her pocket for the yellow cat's eye she had kept.

"That Pete's?" Papa asked.

Grace nodded as she stared at it in her hand. She would have to start filling in for some of the things Pete used to do.

Papa wiped a hand across his face. He was badly in need of a shave. And just then the train blew its whistle.

"We'll have to write a letter to the Hammonds," Papa said, his voice serious. "Thank 'em proper for all they done. I'm sorry I didn't get to the station in time to say something myself."

"I'll never forget them," Grace said.

"No." Papa patted her knee as the locomotive steamed on. "I don't think you ever will."

The long trip to Cincinnati had begun, the rhythmic *clack-ety clack* of the train already measuring the miles. They talked for a while, but Papa was tired and hungry. He said he had been up all night working a job to get money for the train ticket and offered Grace one of the doughnuts in his paper bag.

Grace didn't dare ask him what kind of work. "Here, Papa, take one of my sandwiches," she offered in turn, opening the box beside her. She handed him her lunch while she herself peered into the paper bag and selected a doughnut dusted with white sugar.

Papa ate a ham sandwich and a dill pickle and two plain doughnuts, too. Then he leaned his head back against the seat and fell deep asleep, his tweed cap slipping down over his eyes.

Outside, the countryside rolled by. Grace found she was neither hungry nor tired. She put the rest of her doughnut back in the bag for later. There was far too much to think about. Seeing Mama—and her astonished face in Cincinnati! The little boys pulling at her hands to come watch an ornery billy goat. Fluffy kittens in the hayloft. Fiddle lessons at long last . . .

And this: a starlit summer night with her family gathered on Uncle Fritz's porch steps. Papa has finished tuning his fiddle, and it rests on a stool beside him. Now he leans in close to the radio, as they all do, Grampa Schmidt cupping his ear to hear the sound—*crack!*—of a bat hitting a ball. Grace cheers and, meeting her mother's shining eyes, shifts the weight of a baby sister on her knee.

Author's Note

The story of Grace was inspired by a little girl named Betty Dell Stone. Just before Christmas 1932, Betty and her young brothers were temporarily placed in the Children's Emergency Home of the Central Union Mission of Washington, D.C., because their parents could not afford to keep them. It was one of the darkest periods of the Great Depression. Betty's father had lost his job and would be without work for many months to come.

As was the custom, some of the children staying at the mission were invited home for the holidays with more fortunate Washington families. Betty was one of those lucky children. Two well-dressed sisters chose her for a holiday visit to the boardinghouse they helped their family run on Connecticut Avenue. It was a visit that would unexpectedly extend to four years. Betty soon became part of the family, which included a deaf aunt named Grace. But she became especially attached to one of the sisters who had rescued her from the mission, a young woman named Prudence Shannon, who worked as a secretary in the White House during the administration of President Franklin Roosevelt.

Although Betty was returned to her parents in 1936, she and Miss Shannon remained in touch, with visits and letters back and forth, all of their long lives. Betty grew up and made homes throughout the world with her Air Force husband. She had children and grandchildren, and today lives in a small town outside Atlanta, Georgia.

Meanwhile, Miss Shannon, after Betty's departure, eloped with a young lawyer living in her family's boardinghouse, continued her career at the White House, and eventually went on to have a family of her own. She had three sons, the youngest of whom I married in 1983.

I would like to point out to my readers that although Betty was the inspiration, the story of Grace is largely fiction, with the exception of period details and the few references to President and Mrs. Roosevelt. The latter come directly from the personal journal my mother-in-law kept by neatly typing up remembrances of each day on White House stationery.

Prudence Shannon (Frece) and Betty Stone (Stults) 1933

Prudence Shannon Frece and Betty Stone Stults were exceptional people who lived through extraordinary times. It has been my privilege to know them both.